Crooked Miles, Woven World

Crooked Miles, Woven World

A Novella & Short Stories

by Bruce Henricksen

Lost Hills Books | Duluth, MN

Lost Hills Book
Duluth, MN
www.losthillsbks.com

Published by:

Lost Hills Books
P.O. Box 3054
Duluth, MN 55803
www.losthillsbks.com

Layout: Aaron Bosanko, Sheldon Print & Design, Duluth, MN

Cover art: glass work by Dan Neff and Steven Selchow

Printing: BookMobile, Minneapolis, MN

ISBN-13: 978-0-9798535-8-6

Other Fiction by Bruce Henricksen

Ticket to a Lonely Town
(Stories)

"This wonderful collection... carries us to exquisitely lonely places, the place of childhood, of lost loves."

ANTHONY BUKOSKI, AUTHOR OF *TIME BETWEEN TRAINS*

"Bruce Henricksen is a brilliant stylist, a Nabokov with street smarts, and his command of the language in these stories is a constant pleasure."

BARTON SUTTER, AUTHOR OF *THE REINDEER CAMPS*

After the Floods
(Novel)

"Loss and recovery—and healing—are themes that drive the plot, as people create new lives, crows and dogs converse, and time itself expands and shrinks. It's magical realism... lyrical, funny, sad and thoroughly engaging."

CONNIE WANEK, AUTHOR OF *ON SPEAKING TERMS*

"Henricksen brings such fey charm to this spiritual comedy, with tender feeling for all of his searchers... It's a short, thoroughly enjoyable flight of fancy, filled with sweet wisdom about the way we lean on—and crash into—one another."

SUSAN LARSON, NEW ORLEANS *TIMES-PICAYUNE*

Paul Decker

Preface & Acknowledgments

The novella that begins this collection is published here for the first time. In other stories, characters and situations from pieces published in the past and set elsewhere have been summoned from their graves, given new names and outfits, and spirited off to Duluth, MN.

A lonely man who originally wandered the New Orleans French Quarter, now reincarnated, lives in Duluth and visits Canal Park each Saturday, the donkey-drawn carriage he hired in New Orleans replaced by a yellow moped from *RJ Sports*. A dog that was lost down South after Hurricane Katrina now has a suspicious resemblance to a stray found in Duluth after our city's recent disaster, the Flood of 2012. The man and the dog have adapted well to their new lives at the tip of Lake Superior, believing these to be the only lives they've had. Mums the word.

Magazines that have published my earlier work include Arts & Letters, Briar Cliff Review, Folio, Minnetonka Review, New Orleans Review, North Dakota Quarterly, Pacific Review, Southern Humanities Review, and Tulane Review. I thank them.

I wish to thank Charles Baxter for his provocative book on the art of fiction, Burning Down the House, and Jonathan Gottschall for The Story Telling Animal, his discussion of the crucial role of story in human life. And thanks to my old friends, Ted Cotton and Barton Sutter, for their ongoing encouragement concerning my writing and so much else. A new friend, Roxanne

Sadofsky, read the present manuscript in entirety and offered useful comments and suggestions. And many thanks to Patrick Green, web master and computer guru, and to Aaron Bosanko for layout and design.

I have no idea who I would be without my wonderful wife, Viki, and her ever-present intelligence and goodness. I've also been enriched over the years by the friendship of Paul Decker, my pal from grad school days in Los Angeles. This book is dedicated to him.

NOVELLA

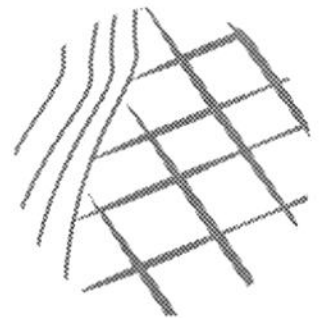

Miranda and the Argonauts

And the heroes breathed again after their chilling fear, beholding at the same time the sky and the expanse of sea spreading far and wide. For they deemed that they were saved from Hades.

The Voyage of the Argo: Argonautica,
Appollonius Rhodius

It was as though Peter thought you could convert clay to gold, like he believed in alchemy. That's how Frederick saw his brother's aspirations, his journey to the East, not the East of the Buddha but the East Coast of the United States. Frederick wanted adventure too. He didn't know where to look for it, but he wouldn't have to look. Soon he would stumble upon it where it haunted the hills close to home. Peter had caught a plane to Boston, attended college and then joined a glittering, newly minted crew of twenty-somethings tumbling like coins into the slot machines of high finance in New York. Frederick stayed in Duluth, waiting.

To Frederick's mind, at least in his less generous moments after shoveling clay all day, there were Peters everywhere—in Minneapolis, in Madison, in Paris and Dubai—Peters living the Madoff, wearing silk shirts and dining where black-coated waiters mince and bow. Peters lighting cigars, speaking knowingly of bundling and options. Peters who are casual on Casual Friday, who join Athletic Clubs and mingle at Happy Hour, who marry manikins that smear or break if you touch them. Frederick stayed in Minnesota, wearing his steel-toed work boots, driving his old Subaru, and imagining the saga of risk, reward, and romance in the fast lane that Peter was writing himself into.

"That world is a perfect storm," their father, a blunt, plank-shouldered man, said one evening as he helped himself to a second baked potato. "It'll either kill him or toss him back on our shore."

"Peter will grow through it on the *inside,*" their mother, Bonnie, replied. She had a way of ducking her head a bit and leveling her gaze to drive a point into a reluctant head. "He'll come back on his own, no storm needed." The father, Ben, usually focused his mind on the outer weather, the mother on the inner. Together, they managed a balanced view of human behavior.

Frederick enrolled in a few classes at the university in Duluth, worked with Ben at *Arrowhead Clay,* and developed his own skills as a ceramicist, sculpting small animals and human figures. Like Peter, he had dreamed of departures, but his dreams were vague and nomadic. One such dream had prompted him some years back to run away from home and spend two nights in a forest with the owls and rabbits. As rain drops pattered on the leaves above, he had imagined he was a fish gazing up at the underside of lily pads. Then he went home. He was eleven.

His second restlessness began on the chilly day in April—he was twenty—when Frederick scrambled from his pickup truck as it began to sink, tires spinning, into mud by the estuary. It only went down a couple of feet, and the rope his dad tossed him may not have been necessary. But the event had been unsettling. And his restlessness grew on the afternoon two weeks later when he cracked a bone in a foot by dropping a fifty-pound box of clay on a work boot that failed in its duty. In addition to mining clay at the estuary, he mixed and boxed it in the warehouse.

So throughout his college years his reservations about a life in the family business grew in lock-step with his increasing responsibilities each summer. But he prided himself in not having followed Peter by dreaming of realms of wealth and sophistication like golden constellations just beyond the hills that bordered their Duluth neighborhood of Gary. Frederick was needed at home. Bonnie, who had personed the gallery and bookstore for years, was facing knee-replacement surgery, so an assistant named Martha Gardener had been hired. And Frederick would stick around.

Martha, twenty-two, had just moved to Duluth after three years of study in drawing and painting on the West Coast. She was, and is, a pretty black woman with a smile as wide as The Milky Way and skin like coffee with cream. Frederick imagined saying that to her, and perhaps her smile and skin, as well as his mother's surgery, kept him on the scene.

As they became friends, Martha talked about her great grandparents, who had moved from land near Monroe, Louisiana to Milwaukee in the back of a pickup truck in 1940. Like so many blacks of that period, they had decided that facing the unknown North was better than remaining in a caste system to be oppressed and perhaps beaten or killed.

"My Louisiana ancestors were share croppers but not Gardeners—the Gardener wing was added in Wisconsin. I don't think you folks up here on the Laurentian Shield understand how brutal it was down South."

She was speaking to Frederick one afternoon as they sipped Cokes on the steps of the gallery beneath the *Feat of Clay* sign. Frederick propped himself against a rail to face her as she spoke. Her cheekbones were strong, and the skin of her face glowed as from an inner light. *Maybe the cheekbones emit light*, he thought.

"The separation of the races was utter," she said, "separate elevators and stairs in public buildings, for Christ's sake. Your feet couldn't tread where white feet had gone, and you could be lynched for plucking an orange from a tree. Lynchings were advertised ahead of time and drew crowds. The atmosphere was carnivalesque. America lynched blacks while the Nazis gassed Jews.

"Granny Indiana used to talk about how the black kids would get the white kids' discarded school books with missing pages and obscene drawings, 'new' books for blacks that ignored their own history. Your education would be white faces gazing back at you from torn pages." She paused to examine a troop of ants traversing the porch step, on some small migration of their own. "And those who had gone North would visit back home in fancy clothing and straightened hair to tell tales about how wonderful and important their lives had become. The Great Migration was driven by violence and pipe dreams."

Frederick told her about his relatives who fled Germany in the 1930's to end up in North Carolina. "It's strange where roots lead when you look under the surface," he said.

"And strange how they entangle with other roots," she added. "History is a rhizome."

"How are you finding Duluth?" he asked.

"I like the size, population-wise, but I'm surprised at all the old brownstone. I thought there'd be more glass and steel, more upward reach."

"Yeah, the city has a thing about keeping the buildings low. Now there are plans for an eleven story office building downtown...big controversy. I imagine Sunday sermons: *The sky was not meant to be scraped!* But things change. You hear more foreign accents these days, from Asia and from the Middle East. We even have a cab driver who speaks Somali."

"My God! Just like New York."

"Never been," Frederick confessed. "No desire."

"Any street gangs in Duluth?"

"Well, we haven't avoided the present completely.

There are some drug dealers transplanted from Chicago, and there's a Native American gang spread out around the state. They call themselves Native Mob. They've been more of a problem in the Twin Cities, but there was a stabbing around here recently too. And we have our very own head shop called *The Last Place on Earth*. People complain about seeing drop-out types sparking and getting tuned up on the downtown sidewalks. The police try to shut it down, but they can't prove that the synthetic stuff actually contains banned substances."

"Easy fix," she said. "Write the laws to address the *effects* of the substance, not its composition."

"Brilliant!"

"Elementary."

"Anyway," Frederick said, draining his Coke and wrapping things up. "Duluth is the real world... in miniature. But let's get back to work." They were preparing the showroom for a local artist's opening that evening.

"Yes, master," she replied through her Milky Way smile, "but don't step on the ants." They were still about their business on the porch. "Ants have a great work ethic. I admire them."

The local artist they were hosting happened to be my wife, Viki Day, whose functional dinner ware and vessels did well, and still do, in gift shops such as *Art Doc* in Canal Park, where tourists go for regional crafts. My interest in Frederick's story owes much to Viki. Her opening at *Feat of Clay* would be part of the Crossing Borders Crafts Tour, an event held each June in which craftspeople up and down the Northshore receive tourists in their studios. The borders in question are two or three county lines, and a brochure with a map is available each year. Many people come up from the Twin Cities to combine the tour with hiking or fishing.

*

The Serafin family had moved to Minnesota from Sanford, North Carolina during the Great Depression. The man who fled the oppression in Germany lost his life in an accident in a brick factory in Sanford. He had worked the giant kilns. Now, for decades in Minnesota, his grandson's family had leased land along the St. Louis River Estuary from which they mined clay.

The red clay the area yielded, red thanks to the proximity of the Mesabi Iron Range, was similar to the red clay from which the ancestor had made bricks so long ago in the South. But red clay had only limited use for potters and ceramicists in Minnesota, so *Arrowhead Clay* also imported from distant regions, the most distant being England, which produced excellent white clay. Around the time of the American Revolution, the British craftsman Josiah Wedgwood had sought to acquire white clay from North Carolina, then called Cherokee clay, for his porcelain creations, but eventually white clay was discovered in Cornwall. Now, in one of history's many reversals, it's exported to America—and to *Arrowhead Clay.*

People who work in clay constitute a network. Frederick's father, Ben, liked to joke that his company's place in that network kept the ocean-going "salties" afloat on the Great Lakes. *Arrowhead Clay* also sold glazes, tools, and books. A showroom, *Feat of Clay*, featured the work of ceramic artists and potters in Minnesota's Arrowhead region, and a studio offered classes in throwing and hand-building.

In the old days, Gary-New Duluth had been the home of a mill run by *U.S. Steel*. Its workers lived in Morgan Park, a company town built by JP Morgan. The town still exists although the steel mill is long gone. Frederick remembered the song his grandfather had sung with the line *My name is Morgan, but it ain't JP*, a song his granddad always followed with a lecture on how the rich are out to fleece the rest of us. But things change. Gary and Morgan Park had become home to golf enthusiasts, kayakers, and even a precious few who might splurge for tickets to the new playhouse, *Wise Fool Shakespeare*, in downtown Duluth, a place Frederick's literature teacher at UMD encouraged him to visit.

When Frederick announced his intention to see a play one evening, his father, whose literary tastes were stuck on movies with Tom Cruise, responded with a snort. "You go for that dreamy stuff, don't you?" he said. Frederick turned on a heel and walked out the door in what his dad later called a huff. It was a friendly sporting event in the Serafin home, The Snorts vs. The Huffs. Ben's snorts were usually accompanied by a smile that sent creases out across his cheeks. I liked him, a soft heart wrapped in a power-lifter's body. I'm sorry he moved away, but I'll get to that later. On the evening of the snort and the huff, Frederick scrubbed off the clay, found a clean shirt, and took Martha to see *The Tempest*.

"I'm glad they cast a black actor for Caliban, that *thing of darkness*," she said as they left the theatre. "It lifted the veil on something in the play." Unconsciously, she touched her own skin.

"Lifted it and smacked you in the face," Frederick replied. "I guess Shakespeare wasn't immune to the prejudices of his day. There's also that play about the Jew."

"No one's free of prejudice, white man," she said, giving him a friendly poke in the ribs.

This was the summer when posters and billboards criticizing "white privilege" had sprouted like mushrooms throughout the city. They usually depicted a white face, thirty-something, scrubbed, and bland, gazing happily down on a Duluth street. Words below the face were to the effect that racism flies under white people's radar. These billboards vied for attention with those claiming that *St. Luke's Hospital* "puts the patient above all else," that *Grandma's Saloon and Grill* serves delicious walleye, and that fetuses can smile—the latter prompting Martha to wonder what in the womb they would smile at.

Two

The evening at the theatre pulled Frederick's mind out of the estuary and the clay, dusted it off, and set it down in a new place. He took the following day off, leaving Martha to work *Feat of Clay* on her own. It was the middle of June. Another dreary spring had made way for another reluctant summer, and after days of rain the weather on Lake Superior finally seemed to beckon. He pulled out a faded wet suit, pulled the old kayak out of the shed and onto the roof of the old Outback, and drove through the downtown tunnels of I-35.

Continuing along London Road toward the beach, Frederick contemplated the elegant Victorian homes overlooking the lake. Among them, in another sort of home, *Lakeside Home*, Frederick's grandmother had died over a decade ago. During his visits, she had described memories that became increasingly small and inaccessible over the weeks, like islands in a rising sea, in a tempest. Sometimes a smile would float over her face only to capsize. And he remembered the human forms slumped in wheel chairs in the halls like broken vessels on a potter's wheel, people convalescing from life by leaving it, sinking slowly into their own dark waters.

He parked at the eastern end of Brighton Beach, unloaded the kayak with its duct-taped repairs, and wrestled it down the path to the Lake Superior shore. After finding a launch site among the rocks that catacomb the shoreline, he paddled eastward. Weather changes quickly on the Northshore, and the clouds that rumbled in like boulders over the northern hills meant trouble.

The wind increased. Frederick fought the bucking water while scanning the shore for a safe harbor, but the kayak went under as waves shattered like glass against the rocks separating lake from land. As the water receded he heard voices...*he's awakening...let him arrive slowly...can you hear me?* The music of violins seeped from a brown wall, the grain of its wood seeming to flow like honey. A human form floated into view.

"I'm Preston Morgan. I live here. And this is Dr. Graves. You've been here since yesterday, and he's been looking after you. He says you've been very fortunate, but he wants to examine you now." Frederick nodded vaguely, and another form approached the bed. His face was narrow, and long sideburns placed his eyes in parentheses.

"So," the doctor said, "you've been z-rayed, and we found nothing broken. Can't say that for your kayak... just toothpicks and tatters now. And old duct tape. You had some nasty bruises and gashes. I dressed them with my own concoction, something to accelerate healing. I must patent it someday. Anyhow, sit up please and slip off those jammies." Frederick complied. "Good, you're already healing nicely. Say how many fingers I'm holding up...and now just follow my penlight with your eyes...Excellent. Now stand up and walk around."

Frederick wobbled a bit at first, pausing at the foot of the bed to grip a post. A purple lizard and a red rose, both crafted from glass, rested on a table near the window. The lizard gazed vacantly at Frederick.

"Go ahead and climb into some of the clothing that Mr. Morgan laid out for you. Let me see how you do." For slacks, there was a choice between standard issue Dockers or blue jeans, but beside them was an extended family of silk shirts with subtle floral designs, of neckties, and of woolen socks. The floor offered a choice between suede loafers and sneakers in Frederick's size. Frederick stood on one foot for the Dockers and reached an arm backward and into a green sleeve with a blue stripe. All went well.

"Good," Doctor Graves said, "with that, I pronounce you on the mend. We won't have to recycle you just yet. Drink plenty of water. I've put three different kinds of bottled water on your night table, each of them pure. It's odd, don't you think, that there are so many kinds of purity? Anyway, I live here in Argo, so if you have any problems let someone know. I'll be with you pronto." He picked up a leather bag like those carried by doctors in old movies, pausing to direct his parenthetical eyes out the window. "I love a summer day by a lake," he exclaimed. "It always makes one feel like buying night crawlers, don't you think?" With that, he retreated through a large, oak door.

"He isn't nearly as morbid as his name might imply for people who plan to be buried," Preston said.

"Not morbid at all," Frederick agreed. "But did he say 'z-rayed'?"

"Yes. X-rays are so yesterday here at Argo."

"What is Argo?"

"My father's name is Jason, and he's a man who likes to pursue a theme—you know about Jason and the Argonauts?"

"Something about looking for gold?" Frederick ventured.

"Yes, the Golden Fleece. We have a yacht, Argo CXIV, in a little harbor among the rocks, and our maintenance man saw you tumble in. He said your blood spattered like paint from Jackson Pollock's brush. That's pretty clever, don't you think? Anyway, here you are." Preston smiled from under a bale of blond hair. His skin was pale, but his dark eyes arrested the tendency toward albino.

"This room is beautiful," Frederick said, looking about slowly. The chandelier opened downward like a giant blossom with pistils and stamens glowing in gently modulating purples, greens, and oranges. The effect was a little like that of a ballroom in an old movie. A fragrance drifted amid the continuing whisper of violins.

Frederick stepped to the window and gazed out at a hedge-lined driveway slanting up a hill to the house for half a mile and then dividing to circle a fountain that featured a spouting, two-story Neptune. Lawns, gardens, and walkways meandered for hundreds of yards on either side of the fountain, and the entire area was populated with sculpture in marble or bronze. Further off, seen from between trees, was the lake, its scrolling waves. "My God," he gasped. Preston Morgan stood beside him.

"We brought you up to the third floor for the view,"

Preston said. "I always think that the morning sun makes the clouds look like rare fabrics, like Chinese silks from the Zhou and Han Dynasties, and like Indian silks from Pochampally. It's a dream come true."

"The blue and white sky is like Chinese porcelain to me," Frederick said.

"Well, I'm a silk freak. Anyway, Argo," Preston went on, "is modeled on Windsor Castle, although we're a bit smaller. Dad has been...well, successful. He likes it here because the city of Duluth once had the highest rate of millionaires per capita in America. Iron mining and lumbering, I guess."

"Fishing, too," Frederick added, "but it's all gone now...But I've lived in Duluth all my life. Why haven't I heard of your...place?"

"A cloak of invisibility helps Dad pursue his projects. He says we need to move forward, not look back. He wants Argo always to be one world ahead of...other worlds. Anyway, over that hill out there to the east we have a nine-hole golf course. It was put in two years ago, and we may go ahead and add another nine. But frankly, it doesn't get much use. I'd like us to play today. What better way to shake off a shipwreck than with a bit of friendly competition?"

"I don't know," Frederick began. "Maybe I should ..."

"Dad wouldn't hear of your leaving so soon. He loves to get to know people washed up on our shore. He can hardly wait for the next storm. And my sister wants to meet you too. You must at least stay another night, and I'll get you home tomorrow."

"My family is already worried, and ..."

"It's been taken care of. We called them and said you are fine after a minor mishap and will be our guest."

"But how did you know . . ?"

"Vee have our vays," Preston said in a mock German accent, "and besides, you were carrying ID. Your stuff is in the wardrobe." He indicated the largest piece of its kind Frederick had ever seen. "Let's go down for some breakfast, and then head for the course."

The spiraling staircase was flanked on one side with paintings of old men in suits (latter day Argonauts?), while the other side offered a view of the hall below, where a marble satyr stood on its only leg. The young men passed a doorway on the second floor landing, which Preston said opened into the library.

"I could show you the library sometime if you're interested. We have a large collection of rare books and manuscripts. Dad's newest prize is the Ellesmere Manuscript from the *Huntington Library* in San Marino. It's the oldest manuscript of Chaucer's *Canterbury Tales*. The margins are illuminated with colored gargoyles and stuff, kind of like a graphic novel. They used real flecks of gold in the ink. Dad loaned California some money, and he got the Chaucer as collateral. I don't really know much about old manuscripts."

"No reason you should," Frederick replied. They both smiled.

"Oh Charles!" Preston called as they reached the ground floor. "We'd like some breakfast outside this morning. Could you see to that?"

"Right away, Mr. Morgan." The man called Charles hurried off.

"I've never been called Mister," Frederick said.

"We'll fix that."

They sat beside the steps rising from the driveway that circled the Neptune fountain. In a few minutes Charles arrived with a cart carrying a silver coffee pitcher, porcelain cups and plates, a large bowl of assorted fruit slices, a second bowl containing scrambled eggs, a platter of bacon, a basket of biscuits, and assorted jams. The silverware glistened in the sun, and the glassware was a symphony of color.

"May I serve you, Mr. Serafin, or would you prefer to help yourself?"

"Oh, I'll dig in on my own, thanks," Frederick responded.

"Mr. Morgan's preference as well," Charles said before vanishing behind a mini-bow.

"So," Frederick said, grinning at Preston, "I'm a Mister now." Preston possessed inordinately large blond eyelashes, and his wink was like the down-and-up of an awning. "I know," Frederick said, "you have your vays."

A bird slightly smaller than a helicopter alighted on Neptune's head. "Dad had some wildlife brought in from Africa," Preston explained, "or for all I know from another planet. I don't know what that creature is called."

"Shame on you," Frederick replied. He had begun to feel at ease with his new companion.

From a mile away, portions of the lake appeared in gaps between spruce trees and pine. A freighter nudged its way west toward Duluth, and Frederick wondered idly if it might contain white clay from England. It disappeared beyond trees, and soon the water sealed over its wake like grass reclaiming an abandoned path. As the young men enjoyed their breakfast in the warmth of the sun, Preston explained that the Morgan golf course consisted of replicas of some of the most famous fairways on the professional tour.

"It makes for a beautiful but difficult course. Fortunately, Dad had one of his people create a little help. Our golf balls have built-in GPS. You still have to hit an airborne shot, but if you do the guidance will straighten it out, keep it on the fairway, and add a hundred yards to the tee shots. Oh, and our golf carts track your shot and take you to your ball, no steering necessary. Father calls it a triumph of the will through technology...remote-controlled pleasure."

"Cool," Frederick said. He was becoming accustomed to the wonders of Argo.

"I think Dad should market the whole system, but to him it's too trivial to be worth the effort."

"Right. Why bother to revolutionize golf?"

Charles materialized again by the table to inquire if all was well, and Preston asked him to have two hover carts brought to the fountain. Charles slipped away.

"Miranda will appear from over there in a moment," Preston said, pointing to a place where a path entered the woods. A bouquet of cardinals rose from a maple tree and hovered for a moment before bending westward, and in a few seconds a girl in a white dress emerged from the trees followed by a brown and white faun scarcely old enough to walk.

"How did you know . . ?" Frederick began, but then broke off. "Oh, never mind."

After a few steps the girl paused, knelt, and whispered in the faun's ear. It turned and made its rickety way back into the trees. Then Miranda turned toward Argo, waved, and burst into a run, her bare feet hardly touching the grass, and the thin fabric of her dress, backlit by the sun, revealing a stunningly beautiful body in motion, a body as white as milk. She arrived at the fountain just as did the two golf carts, and Preston and Frederick trotted down the steps to meet her. She wore a rose in her hair.

"You ride with Miranda," Preston said. "Your cart knows to follow mine."

Seated beside Miranda, Frederick found himself gazing at the loveliest woman he had ever seen. She was fair skinned and full lipped, with the rose pinned in hair of auburn and honey. Moreover, she smiled at him in the shy manner that cannot be resisted even if resistance were, for some insane reason, called for. But perhaps I allow my own values to intrude here.

"I'm so happy to meet you," she said.

"I'm happy too."

"Well good. I don't meet many people from the outside. Father monopolizes them when they wash ashore. Are all the men as handsome as you? That couldn't be, could it?"

Without instructions from either passenger, the vehicle, which had no wheels but hovered a foot or so in the air, purred its way to the course, following Preston's along a winding sidewalk of inlaid tiles, up a hill, and around various bushes, gazebos, and trees. Frederick recognized a Henry Moore sculpture. He turned to gaze back at Argo, fronted by its massive fountain. The marble mansion, with its many towers and angled parapets and with the orange glow of a hundred windows, was radiant against the green hillside. Argo shimmered like an arpeggio.

"It's alive!" Frederick exclaimed, returning his attention to the vehicle that knew its route exactly.

"Well, Dad's scientists are working on a man-made man. They will laugh, cry, dream...the whole package."

"Programmed laughter?"

"Well, maybe it's beyond programming. I don't know. Anyway, these carts are only radio-operated machinery. The first time we used them, everything was bailing wire. But it's all worked out now."

"Bailing wire?"

"You don't say that?"

"We say 'haywire' sometimes."

Miranda blushed. "You see, I try to talk your language and I only say foolish things."

"I think 'bailing wire' works just fine."

"Can you stay long?" Miranda asked. "I want to keep you here forever, you know." She brushed a lock of hair aside and tipped her head in the way a girl had done once in one of Frederick's steamier dreams.

"Today, I'd stay forever."

"Okay. That's good enough to start."

The golf balls were shooting stars, curving to the center of fairways, bending around doglegs, soaring over water hazards, and landing within a few feet of pins on rolling greens as smooth as silk. Miranda played bare-footed, the many movements of her body only partially veiled by her shear dress. Occasionally, ornately colored birds—yellow warblers, blue birds, cardinals, and gold finches—flashed through the air to alight on her shoulder. She whispered with each visitor, and then it flickered and swooped into the green depth of trees, as if with an urgent message. Preston, his golf ball programmed to leave Frederick and Miranda by themselves, waved and smiled from the far sides of the fairways.

"Please tell me about your life," she asked. "I want to know all about reality. Is it true that things change all the time...the automobiles, the cell phones, the language? It seems like life out there must be a confused search among new gadgets and old, yesterday and tomorrow all shuffled together. Is it like that?"

"Well," Frederick replied, "it's a tough place to get a nap." But he proceeded to tell her about his family's business and about the university, both of which fascinated Miranda in a way that Frederick in turn found fascinating. "I take it you don't get out much," he remarked at one point.

"Out? Oh, I've never been *out*. Argo moves about, but I'm always in it. Argo isn't just here in...this is called

Minnesota? It isn't just here. It's been all over the world, but I've never been out of Argo. I'm always on the ship, a floating world, and I don't really have a home like you do. It's a diaspora without a destination, and it feels as though my life is suspended. I think the Morgans are a lost tribe.

"But tell me about politics. My father always talks about politics, but you need to have been off the ship to understand it. Dad used to work in banking in the real world before he returned to Argo."

Frederick did his best to explain elections and political parties, realizing as he did that he hadn't been enough out of his own kayak to say anything useful.

"Do you believe in equality?" she asked.

"I suppose so."

"It's at the top of Dad's Pantheon of Social Errors. Just so you know."

Then, as they rode down the ninth fairway, Miranda spoke of the small gathering they'd find back at Argo for the lunch hour. "It's old friends and family members that we stay in touch with. We call them the Elders. They're pretty quiet, but don't let it bother you. Their energy levels aren't what they used to be. I'm afraid they're becoming obsolete, just like last year's cell phone in your world."

As they climbed the steps of the mansion, the great doors opened, and the three young people paused at the marble statue in the hall. A plaque identified it as a Satyr of Praxiteles, 4th Century BCE.

"It's on loan from some museum in Rome," Preston

explained. "No one is sure whether it was really done by Praxiteles or by an apprentice. It's hard to care at this point."

"I like having statues and paintings," Miranda said. "They help you feel in touch with distant people and places. Distant times. They make me feel more alive. It's a paradox, I suppose. Dad just likes them for status... status in a world he doesn't even live in."

"Paradoxes grow like shrooms," Preston said. "Let's just look in on the Glass Room before we separate for a little down time. Dad is eager to meet you. He may even invite you to join the team."

They stood in the entrance to the Glass Room, which was peopled, if that was the right word, with what appeared to be a dozen or more manikins. The air was fragrant with flowers, and somewhere violins whispered and yearned. The manikins were randomly placed among pedestals displaying vases and glass statuary. Close to the doorway, an elderly man with pendulous white hair seemed frozen in glistening ice. His arm had stopped short in the gesture of raising a Champaign flute containing an amber cordial. Other Elders seemed to have been conversing, but had also been arrested in mid-sentence or mid-laugh. But for the music, the room held an eerie silence.

As Preston began to explain, Miranda placed a reassuring hand on Frederick's arm. "These are all family members, we call them the Elders, who are either transitioning or who have finished transitioning. I know that your people don't transition. It's what we do instead of dying. We're different. Maybe it was some genetic mutation centuries ago. I don't know. But we don't die, we become glass. For a while, maybe as much as two or three years, a person might have brief spells of paralysis, of glassiness. But over time it becomes more and more permanent. Notice that woman in the ball gown at the far end of the room. She is able to move her head slightly from time to time. Sometimes she utters a sound or two. She may remain like that for another month or more before her transition is complete."

Preston fell silent as Frederick gazed about, Miranda's hand moving gently on his arm. "Oh look," she said, "Father is returning."

In the middle of the room, one of the manikins, a broad-shouldered man of average height, began to move more actively, almost as one might do when stretching after sleep. The manikin looked about, saw the three young people, and smiled politician-style as he approached them. His blue-white hair swirled back in a pompadour like the wake of a lumbering ship, and his skin might have appeared to be Botoxed and lotioned had not its transformation to glass been explained so matter-of-factly. His lapel pin, a purple lizard, seemed incandescent.

"Frederick," Miranda said, "this is my father, Jason Morgan. Dad, here is Frederick Serafin."

"I'm so glad you could join us, Mr. Serafin, although the event that brought you here must have been harrowing. But I see that Dr. Graves has done a good job. These are all family members," he said, gesturing to the room. "I assume our odd mode of being, or of ceasing to be, has been explained." Preston nodded.

"Well," Mr. Morgan said, "I'd like to commune with my Elders for a bit longer, and I imagine you could use a rest after your golf. Lunch will be served outdoors in an hour, and I look forward to talking with you then."

Jason Morgan, whose antique moustache recalled the Belle Époque, executed a miniature bow and walked back to join the frozen others. At that moment, Frederick's attention was caught by motion in the far wall. The three interior walls of the Glass Room were in fact made of glass, and behind them giant sharks cruised. It was as though the room, with its captured manikins, was the tank and the sharks were the curious public. Back by the satyr in the hallway, Miranda continued the explanation.

"When we grow old, we turn to glass. That's why some of those faces looked like...well, tea cups and sugar bowls. Eventually, after our transitions are finished, we break. When we can't be repaired any longer, we are melted down. Those vases and statues you saw on the pedestals...they're all made from people."

"I'm...I need to rest," Frederick said.

"Can you find your room?" Preston asked. "If you're tired from the golf, there are elevators on the far wall." Frederick followed Preston's gaze and saw a black man quickly ascend a narrow stairway near the elevators. "The stair beyond the elevators is for the servants," Preston explained. "We don't use it."

*

In his room, Frederick selected from the three bottles of pure water lined up by the lizard and the rose on the table top. He took the one with a blue label depicting a ship at sea, swallowed its contents, which tingled gently in his throat, and then he settled into bed to doze in a pool of half formed thoughts—the statues outdoors, the glass people indoors but watched by sharks, and the mysterious, one-legged marble faun, here from somewhere beyond veils of time, language, and culture.

Perhaps it was just a smattering of clouds passing outside, but the room seemed to breathe sunlight, inhaling and exhaling. He was awakened by Preston's voice, which hung in the air but came from nowhere in particular.

"Yo, Frederick. You can't see me, but I'm speaking to say lunch is served now. Just tell me if you are okay." As if to refute the elegant radiance of Argo, a wasp buzzed in the bedroom window, frantic to escape into sun and foliage.

"I'm fine, Preston. Be down in a minute."

Frederick saw Preston, Miranda, and Mr. Morgan at a table by the Neptune fountain, where eight or more Kio fish patrolled the shallows beneath a floating mosaic of lily pads. More so than Miranda's or Preston's, Jason Morgan's face reflected the sun like an office window. Frederick had scarcely seated himself, when Morgan began the interview.

"I hope you're not a Christian, Frederick. Christianity is a morality for slaves. It makes a virtue of weakness and poverty, while pretending that wealth and power are sins. The Argonauts are not about Christianity. Are you Christian?" He stroked his moustache thoughtfully. Frederick wondered if it would also turn to glass eventually.

"I don't go to church," Frederick answered, "but I haven't thought much about those things."

"Well fine," Morgan said. "We will help you to think correctly about 'those things,' as you call them." His sentences seemed to be served with a condiment of scorn. "Understand that the Argonauts are above other moralities, and that is because we are above other people. Have you read your namesake, Friedrich Nietzsche? Nietzsche identified a kind of person he called the Ubermensch, or Overman.

"We at Argo are New Overmen, a network that courts anonymity but spans continents. We own fleets and cities. We intend to own the world...the air you inhale...the water you drink. One day we will own the stars. You can also be an Overman, exercising your responsibility to privatize the future. We will teach you to join our journey." He touched his moustache absently.

"Aren't people responsible to each other?" Frederick ventured.

"That's an argument of weaklings who rely on help from others. We will create a future through the power of will."

Morgan tossed a biscuit into the fountain, which the Koi attacked like sharks smelling blood. Frederick glanced at Miranda, who looked away in the direction of the lake—Lake Superior, the Uberlake.

"I don't have a lot of faith in my will power," Frederick said. "If I can't tell my brain to shut up and go to sleep at night, where's the will power? Anyway, who would I be over as an Overman?" His question brought Miranda's eyes back to him.

"Why, you'd be over the inferior races, the inferior minds. You'd be over the lame and the poor, over the sheeple and their disgusting, packed little lives. One step from the toilet to the tub. Six steps from the sofa to the door. Disgustingly equal like ants, a herd of ants. Sheeple and ants. Haven't you noticed that only the weak believe in equality?" He paused as a waiter with Asian features topped-up their water glasses and then limped away.

"Here at Argo...and we have Argos in 23 countries now...at Argo we are about world domination. It will be a demanding task, organizing this botched planet with its democracies, theocracies, dictatorships, and oligarchies. And don't forget its filthy little territories run by illiterate teenagers armed with assault rifles and demented by hash." The glass lizard on his lapel glittered in the sun. "Some of us are growing old. I have begun to experience transition myself, and we're engaged in a recruiting effort. I conjured your little storm at sea because I knew that your family provides raw material from which art arises. I like the idea of you being my raw material...my clay. And then perhaps you can use your art to aid our journey."

Huh? Frederick thought, but he said, "And what form would this overness take?"

"We'll talk more at dinner. I want you to enjoy the afternoon and our modest way of life. Feel free to poke around. Check out the library. Visit the glass works.

There's nothing to hide at Argo...once you're here, that is." With that said, Mr. Morgan stood and walked away, his lunch untouched. Miranda brushed away a tear.

"That went well," Preston sighed, "but don't mind Dad. He's a little intense. I apologize, Frederick. I thought he was over that domination stuff, but apparently I was wrong. I'm going to leave you two alone."

Frederick and Miranda finished their lunch and began a walk across the expansive lawn. Near a statue by Giacometti, one of his stick men, they came upon a small man with a bird-like face atop a red vest. He was seated or propped on a marble bench in an advanced state of glassy transition, and Miranda bent down to place her face in front of his eyes. An arm lay in the grass by the bench, one glassy finger broken away from the hand.

"Uncle Ray," Miranda said, "you've had an accident. I'll call the studio right now, and we'll get you repaired."

She stood, pulled a small device similar to a cell phone from a pocket, and pushed a number. She spoke into the air, not the device, and the air answered. "William? This is Miranda. Uncle Ray is on a bench on the front lawn. He's had an accident. Can you come right away? It's an arm, William. Yes, right away. Thank you." Then she knelt again in front of Uncle Ray. "William will be here in a moment. He will make you one again." A sound like the gentlest breeze in grass crossed Ray's lips. "You're welcome, Uncle Ray. We'll wait with you for William. We love you."

Glancing back toward the mansion, Frederick

noticed two uniformed men rounding the corner of the building and approaching a parked vehicle. One may have been wearing a sidearm.

Miranda gazed into the sky. "Are they scudding, the clouds?" she asked. "How do you scud if you're a cloud?"

"You need to move faster. Those are just lazing clouds."

"You need to be haul-ass clouds. Isn't that an expression, *haul-ass?*"

"Yes," Frederick said. "Perfectly serviceable."

"You teach me so much." A man in jeans and a baseball cap approached in a hovering vehicle that resembled a large wine bottle, its glass doors opening upward like wings. "William! I'd like you to meet Frederick Serafin. He's from out there."

"I heard about your accident," William said, extending a hand. "Luckily, you don't seem to need my services. Of course you wouldn't."

"Speaking of which," Miranda said, nodding toward Uncle Ray.

"Yes," William said. "Let me help you into the ambulance, Uncle Ray. Careful now. That's it. We'll fasten the seat belt and then fly slowly. We don't want you bouncing about and cracking."

As Miranda and Frederick continued their walk, Miranda suggested that they might visit the glassworks where people were repaired or ultimately melted down. "Once transition is finished and you start to break a lot, you're melted down, sort of like cremation in your world, only our dead are used to make statues and blown-glass art objects. I think it's comforting, knowing you'll still be in the world as something beautiful, don't you?"

"I do," Frederick said uneasily, "although I think I'd rather just walk outside today."

"Blown glass is nice, but it's a dangerous art, too. Melted glass can do a lot of harm. It must be wonderful to shape cool, moist clay with your bare hands, to make it rise into something beautiful. Hey, are you limping from yesterday's shipwreck?"

"No, I dropped a box on my foot a few weeks ago. Maybe you have clay here. Shall we have a look around? Is there a creek or a river nearby?"

"What a wonderful idea! Follow me!" She was off, her bare feet flying and her auburn hair rising on the breeze.

Fifty yards into the woods, a creek whispered over rocks and along a shallow bank that Frederick examined. Unfortunately, although the ferns were lovely, there was no clay. They continued to walk beside the creek as birds darted and squirrels scampered. Fingers of sunlight played in the leaves of trees. Eventually they came to a gazebo and sat. There the sunlight was broken glass fallen through the leaves and scattered on the ground. The branches of a willow bent down to touch the stream, perhaps to listen to the water's whisper. A great blue heron, balanced and still on a single leg like the Satyr of Praxiteles in the hall, eyed them from the far side of the creek.

"I don't know what to say about Dad. It's true that he has some sort of network, other Argos that we visit.

But I have no idea how serious they are about world domination. Sometimes I think they're just old people entertaining themselves, casting themselves as heroes in a story by Homer. Do people do that over on your side?"

"All the time," Frederick said. "Everyone talks about his life... or hers...as though he has the starring role in some epic. Everyone is the star of his own life. Maybe that's why memory is so unreliable. It needs to be rewritten to keep the person in the starring role. No one wants to be Robin when you could be Batman." This is how he'd felt about his brother writing himself into a heroic tale of high finance.

"Dad will be perfectly normal for weeks, and then this other person springs out of his head like a Jake-in-a-box. All the talk about his 'journey.' Journeys are the stuff of stories too, aren't they? It's hard to know what's in a mind."

"A mind under bad influences ..."

"Or a mind left to itself," she broke in eagerly. "It grows wild. When I was at Argo-by-Kyoto I learned about the art of Japanese gardens. The gardener uses a technique called *shakkei,* which means "borrowed scenery." It refers to how the view of a distant mountain or body of water can be framed and presented by angles of vision built into the garden. The outside becomes part of the inside. The mind's garden also borrows scenery, but the mind needs its gardener to make the borrowings lovely.

"Our journeys, our literal ones, are educational though. Did you know that in Malaya they eat bird's-nest soup? We had it at Argo-by-Kuala Lumpur. The swiftlets' nests are difficult to find, only high in the mountains. They're a delicacy. And when the people show fireworks, it isn't about war and explosions; it's about making 'smoke flowers.' And your silly Juliet thought that there's nothing in a name! Journeys teach you things.

"But maybe learning things like that is just collecting mental junk, just filling for my little story. I don't know. Dad's mind is a storage locker with a bit of mythology, a scrap of philosophy, and an interest in world trade... just stuff tossed together. He doesn't talk *with* anyone, just to them. I think that when people really talk they reach into each other to help shape something inside her...or him. They become gardeners. We shape each other when we talk, don't you think? It makes us social."

"I hadn't thought of it that way, but yes. You shape me today, although you won't get me to eat a bird's nest. I draw the line at puppies."

"Now you're pulling my foot!" she said, laughing.

They spoke for an hour, and then Miranda touched his hand. "I need to go to the library now," she said. "Father insists that I study every afternoon from three o'clock to five. These days I'm doing differential calculus and organic chemistry. Home schooling, isn't that what you say?" As they stood, the heron rose into the air, beads of water trailing from its feet.

"Yes," Frederick said, "I had organic chem at the university. We called it 'Orch'—carbon, hydrogen, and oxygen ..."

"The triumvirate of organic matter," Miranda said, "although I think the Morgans must have picked up some silicon along the way."

"Ah, that would explain it."

They followed the path through the trees until it opened onto the lawn, and then they passed Neptune, with the Kio fish cruising at his feet. They climbed the marble steps and paused by the satyr in the hall. Miranda gestured toward its missing foot. "Poor Bambi," she said, "breaking just like the rest of us."

"Bambi," Frederick repeated. "Strange how a word can transform something."

"Yes, like the word 'smoke flowers'. It's magic," she said, and then went on. "But Father likes to have us seated for dinner by 6:45. Shall we meet here at 6:30? Here by Bambi?" She stroked the blue sleeve of Frederick's, or Preston's, silk shirt. "There's a billiard room down that hall. Preston is a fanatic. If he hears the click of balls, he's certain to materialize at your side with a cue in hand. Oh, and tell me if you prefer flesh, fish, or foliage for dinner... Good, we agree. I'll let the staff know. I must run!"

*

Dinner occurred under an epic chandelier at a long mahogany table with elaborately fluted edges and sculpted legs. Portraits on the walls, most likely of Elders, lent the room a chilly atmosphere of surveillance. Charles seated people according to a predetermined plan, placing Frederick across from Miranda, who had arrayed herself in an exotic palette of burnt sienna, cadmium red, and Indian yellow, a palette that defied the somber authority of the portraits.

When the three young people were seated, Uncle Ray was carried in by two servants, apparently Latinos, and placed beside Miranda, his black suit-coat nearly slipping down around fragile shoulders. He wore a red tie.

"Dad always has at least one Elder at the table with us," Preston whispered to Frederick.

"Uncle Ray! It's so good to see you whole again!" Miranda exclaimed. "William is a miracle worker!"

Both of Ray's arms hung at his sides, and his small, avian head bent forward. He might have seemed to pray, but given the militantly secular atmosphere of Argo, one should probably say that Uncle Ray examined the table. In any case, he was motionless.

Next, Mrs. Morgan was carried in like a life-sized porcelain doll in a blue evening gown, its upper rim adorned with crystals. "And here is Mother. Frederick, you haven't met my mother yet, Edith Morgan. Mother, this is my new friend, Frederick."

"I'm pleased to meet you, Mrs. Morgan," Frederick said. She sat erect with pale blue eyes like delicate pearls. Her right hand, frozen in the middle of a gesture, or perhaps on its way to attend to a lock of hair, carried the largest diamond Frederick had ever seen. The smallest breath escaped her lips painted a pearly pink to commune with her eyes. Frederick wondered if makeup artists were employed for the people in transition.

"Hello, Mother." Preston offered the greeting mechanically.

Jason Morgan was the last to enter, seating himself authoritatively at the head of the table. Miranda and Frederick had both ordered vegetarian. A fish with glazed eyes, lying on its side next to sprigs of asparagus and a lemon slice, was placed in front of Mrs. Morgan and another was served to Preston. Uncle Ray stared down at a Chateaubriand, which was also Mr. Morgan's selection. Charles, the usual towel draped over an arm, poured wine into glittering glasses (made from ancestors?), Pouilly-Fuise to accompany the fish and the vegetarian entrees, and a darker burgundy to accompany the Chateaubriand. Salad and cheese would be served last, European style.

Mr. Morgan said hello to each person individually, referring to his daughter as Admired Miranda, and then, smoothing his moustache with the small finger of his left hand, he began his speech:

"I want to clarify some points that were introduced at lunch. I want you to know, Frederick, that I intend to control the world. My colleagues have convinced the Supreme Court of the United States that money is speech and that corporations are people. Never mind how we did that. Elections will now be controlled by the Overmen, and we are they. We are...to acquire the culture...investments in the film industry...eliminate liberal...and book publishers ...under our ownership... television and radio." His speech had slowed and become disconnected, a road of ever more potholes. He paused to sip his wine. "This...not just America... the world...ours." The flesh of his face had begun to harden. "We...post-citizenship...post-factual...only perspectives...no values... no guilt ..." His hand moved slowly toward his fork. "No self...hood...only deeds... over...come the past. Life ceases...in repose...exists in the moveo...the motio...the go from past to fu ..." His sounds, which had been bumps in a road, became reports from a pistol, each report making his face twitch and recoil. Harden.

He tried to sample his Chateaubriand, but his hand froze on the way to his mouth, matching the arrested gesture of his wife. The slice of meat remained impaled on his fork through many long minutes before slipping off onto the table. Uncle Ray stared into his plate, his head cocked like that of a robin listening for a worm. Charles limped about, refilling glasses and removing plates. The stern Elders stared from their frames, and salad was served in Arctic silence.

Eventually the young people left the room, Frederick pausing in the doorway to glance back at the strange tableau of elegant, crystallized madness. They stopped by the satyr dubbed Bambi to examine one another with troubled eyes and then to talk.

"That is the first time Dad has frozen up twice on the same day," Miranda said.

"I'm frightened," Preston confessed. And, with a tremor in his cheek and his voice, he did indeed appear frightened. "I...I won't know what to do if everything falls to me. I don't want it."

"You'll be wonderful," Miranda said. "You're my wonderful brother, and you'll make me proud."

"Please, Frederick," Preston said, "I had thought that we'd just give you a pleasant vacation here. I'm so sorry, but inside I'm like you were on the outside when you arrived yesterday. I feel battered and need to be alone." With that, he left.

"See me in the morning?" Miranda's voice sought a tone of brightness belied by her tears. "I go out early to be with my friends. Come early to the gazebo by the creek, and you'll meet them." She moved close to him and brushed his face with her lips. "I feel so alone sometimes." Then she was gone.

That night, as he tried to sleep or at least to focus only on his breathing, phantoms rode the melodies of invisible violins. Tuxedoed servants hovered like black moths about a gigantic chandelier. A one-legged satyr danced. Books burst into flames, and gold and purple gargoyles leapt from the margins of manuscripts. A woman seated at a table began to melt. Glass figurines pointed from shelves, whispering, "those are pearls that were her eyes." A clown named Jake sprang screaming from a coffin in an open grave. Doors turned to honey and flowed across the floor. Frederick was drowning.

He rose early in the morning, choosing the blue jeans and the sneakers this time, and made his way quietly down the stairs, past Bambi, and out to the walkway leading to the gazebo. Before entering the arbor, he paused to look back at Argo with the morning sunlight melting down its columns and parapets. A large white pine leaned toward an outer wall as though eavesdropping on the intrigues within. There had been rain during the night, and a few huddled clouds were marooned in the distant hills.

Then he found the gazebo in the trees where the willow touched the water. The blue heron, contemplative and still, had returned to the place it had occupied yesterday. Miranda wore a white skirt and a necklace of colored glass—pieces of a relative? A rose nestled in her hair. She sat in the grass stroking a faun resting its head in her lap. Nearby, a leopard and a unicorn lay together, while finches and bluebirds darted among the branches overhead.

"These are my friends," Miranda said, "so they can be your friends too."

"Do they have names?"

"No, we don't need names here in the forest. Names only point to differences, but here we are one happiness."

She reached into a basket, withdrew an apple, and cut it in half. "Help the unicorn and the leopard share this apple. Then you'll be their friend, too." Frederick took the halves and sat down beside the resting animals, and Miranda began to hum a melody that seemed like the song of a bird at once strange and familiar. A response trilled from the far side of the creek.

"I'd want you to sing always," he said. Martha's image had faded in his mind. Perhaps Proteus, the ancient sea-god of change, had placed a hand on his heart.

"Want me to sing if..?" When he did not reply, she said, "I worry about Father, and when you worry about Father you worry about everything. Sometimes he's Prospero, but other times he's Caliban...the thing of darkness. Have you read that play by Shakespeare? Anyway, a mind left to itself can go bad."

"I'm sorry he's unwell. Maybe it will pass."

"It will only pass when he transitions further, and then things will fall to Preston...and to me a bit, too. Argo will be ours, and we will need to deal with the other Morgans in all the other Argos. I don't even know their names."

"And do you believe ..."

"In the vast conspiracy? I don't even know. Dad seems to think that if something is said often enough it becomes fact."

"People behave that way on my side of reality too."

"I wish I lived in your world. I'm fascinated by your interest in clay and sculpture, and by all of the art in your world. Your people make art from so many materials, from clay, stone, metals, paint, fabric, sounds, words. Each art is like an instrument in a huge orchestra." She reached into her basket and tossed bread pieces in the grass for the birds.

"I like clay because it seems like a human medium to me," Frederick said. "It's the human voice in the orchestra. I suppose I'm influenced by that old metaphor that says the flesh is clay. Anyway, you need to be interested in something or other out there. It helps you get through. But the world, reality, is overrated. It's an unstable thing that can shatter like ..."

"Like glass? Like Uncle Ray?"

"Sorry. There's wonderful art made from glass, too. How is Uncle Ray?"

"William and Dr. Graves both report that he's fine today."

The creek rippled among rocks where a floating branch had become lodged, reminding Frederick of his recent accident. "You could come with me," he said. "I'd love you always."

"If I sing?"

"Even when you don't."

"But my friends . . ," she stroked the faun. "The unicorn mated with a deer, and this is his son. See the small horn beginning on his forehead? What would these creatures do in reality, and what would become of me when I begin to be glass?" The silence settled like mist, and then she said, gazing at the roses, daffodils, and nasturtiums, "It's such a sad beauty the flowers have...so delicate and so soon to die."

At that moment Preston arrived. Blue ghosts of a sleepless night crouched under his eyes, and last night's tremor still haunted his face. His thicket of blond hair needed attention. "It's Dad," he said.

"Is he still hardening?" Miranda asked.

"Depends on how you mean it. He's back to normal physically, but he isn't happy." Preston's eyes shifted under his prominent lashes to settle on Frederick. "He's angry that you aren't onboard with his plans... his politics. We need to get you to your home. Dad can be violent, or his people can."

"I'll go too, then," Miranda said. "I'll go to the other world."

"Well," Preston said to Frederick, "in failing the father's test you've passed the daughter's." Then he gazed for a long moment at his sister. "Are you certain about going to reality...working, being a strange creature among...sorry, Frederick...among people who are often unwelcoming and worse. Tell her, Frederick."

Frederick caught his breath like a person drowning. "It would be very hard for you," he told Miranda. "Here you and your animal friends drink goodness from the trees, the creek, and even the stones. It would not be the same in reality." Perhaps he knew then that there are borders that cannot be crossed.

"It hurts you to say it," Preston said, "which proves your honesty. I've found myself wishing we were brothers. But come, we need to go." He motioned for them to stand. "The hover car is being brought to the fountain. Dr. Graves will be there to say goodbye. He's very fond of you, and he also wants to assure himself that his own work has been successful."

Miranda gave the faun a final caress, rolled another apple in the direction of the unicorn and the leopard, and then she stood, hooking her basket to an arm. The heron rose into the air, as though its duty to chaperone were finished. Miranda's face darkened. They followed the path to the edge of the forest and crossed the expanse of lawn to Neptune, whose lips spilled water that created miniature rainbows as it fell to the Kio prowling below. The morning sun, still low, threw shadows of trees and statues across the lawn.

Three armed men by the fountain retreated after a dismissive gesture from Preston. By the fountain, a black servant limped about, sweeping shards of broken glass into a neat pile. Frederick wondered if it was one of the Elders, or even Uncle Ray. Preston and Miranda ignored the servant. Then Dr. Graves approached, placed his medicine bag on the rim of the fountain, and extracted a small bottle. He smiled at Frederick, his brown eyes glittering like copper specks cupped between the parentheses of his sideburns.

"Mr. Serafin, I'm so sorry to hear of your sudden departure. Here is another of my concoctions. It'll help to assure that your healing process hurries to a perfect finish. Please do me the honor of sampling it. It's seriously yummy."

Miranda placed her hand on Frederick's arm and her lips on his cheek. "Please be happy," she said. "I'll always care."

As Frederick drank the doctor's concoction, Miranda became less substantial. The morning sunlight that had shone through the edges of her dress now passed through her body as well. Unstable and nearly asleep, Frederick was carried as though by waves into the hovering vehicle.

He awoke on the ground beside his Subaru at the east end of Brighton Beach. A brown dog of mixed breed separated itself from a pack and approached, tail wagging. Frederick gave him a pat, wondering if it might be a confused stray like himself. The sky was a scribble of bruised clouds ghosting to the east over a shoreline strewn with branches. The lake had turned brown with mud, and a car was planted nose down in a sinkhole, blocking one of the exits to the highway.

Frederick drove slowly back through Duluth, detouring around street damage, rubble, and standing water. He stopped to watch a manhole cover dance atop a brown geyser and then tumble to the pavement. It was impossible to know if the water in the streets was deep enough to damage the car as it surged and struggled through the city.

On Superior Street, the faces of pedestrians on the sidewalk flowed past the car like debris. Although there was no supermarket within a mile, a shopping cart lay on its side against the curb. At *The Last Place on Earth* the synthetic drug trade thrived. Four girls with streaked hair and nose rings, perhaps a coven of Ana worshipers, tried not to scatter in the breeze. Could they have conjured the flood? A few doors down a white-haired man in a trench coat stood on a crate. He wore a sign, but the ink had run and the sign was illegible.

At Lake Avenue Frederick was stopped by a human stream flowing and splashing across Superior Street toward Canal Park. Even had the traffic light been working, it seemed unlikely that the walkers, heading urgently toward a gathering of the disturbed, would have heeded it. Various groups passed in succession like panels in a slide show. A crew of old men carried bath towels, which they flipped over their shoulders in unenthusiastic self-flagellation. Nuns in their official black-and-white swung rosaries, and behind them a black man carried a trumpet and dance-walked as in a jazz funeral. Next, sign carriers pumped the air with scribbled messages tacked to sticks, messages linking the recent disaster to gay marriage and God's wrath. One carrier banged the butt of his stick on the hood of the Subaru, leaving small dents. Then he pushed a grinning face against the driver's window, giving the whole event a nightmarish turn. Watchers lined the sidewalks. Eventually, the flow of humanity thinned to a trickle, and Frederick continued west.

At the next intersection, he recognized a former classmate from Denfeld High School in a car that stopped beside him, windows down and tunes cranked. It turned and squealed uphill, a Just Married message scrawled in red (lipstick?) on its rear window. Whatever had happened to the city had not stopped the marriage. Frederick felt relieved. *That's the Duluth I know.* Eventually, he passed Morgan Park on the left, and finally slowed to a stop at his family's yellow Dutch colonial house in Gary, across the highway from the estuary. Mud and branches had tumbled down the hill and filled the yard, and a soggy newspaper dated three days ago languished on the porch.

Three

Years ago, in my college days, I took a trip to Canada with Viki, my wife-to-be. We went to plays at Stratford and spent a couple of days in Toronto. Crossing into Canada had been easy, and the visit had been golden. But returning home, we were stopped and interrogated at length. I wore a beard and long hair then, and I suppose we just didn't look right to the three uniformed defenders of the border who manned the station. My wife's luggage was searched article by article, and she was asked to describe in detail the uses to which she put some very personal items. It was cruel. My take-away was that it is one thing to cross a border but quite another to return. Maybe that had been the threesome's intended message. I don't know.

Frederick might also have encountered questions upon his return to Duluth, but it was June of 2012. Only a short lull in the rain that had fallen for days had allowed him to take to the lake, and then torrents tumbled down from the hills and through the city. Animals had drowned in the zoo, streets and bridges were washed away, and homes were destroyed. Damage to public property alone in and around the city was estimated at well over 100 million dollars.

Ben grumbled good humoredly about sons who skip town during an emergency, but he was too busy with his clean-up efforts—the basement of the house had flooded—to focus on Frederick's absence. My wife's studio was badly flooded, and regional potters moved about in teams to help one another. For days after the flood, houses groaned and sighed as hidden pressures released and as joints and beams slipped back into place or further out of place. In this atmosphere, Frederick's adventure, except for some quizzical looks from Martha, went under the radar. Nature had provided a muddy cover.

Martha put in extra time at her new cause, the *Safe Harbor Mission*, since the homeless had also taken a hit from the flood. Then, even before the waters subsided, the summer's epic, nation-wide heat wave commenced, including Duluth on its itinerary. Sweltering workers in orange jackets manned jackhammers in the flood-damaged streets, brown thought bubbles of dust drifting over their heads. The evening sky boiled with stars.

Nationwide, the heat resulted in loss of life and in damage to the country's food supply. Global-warming deniers were silenced, the Tea Party put ice in its Lipton, federal disaster dollars shriveled like fried bacon, and the smart money on Wall Street invested green. Frederick and Martha convinced local businesses to chip in for window air-conditioning units at the Mission, and an electrician volunteered to do the 220 volt wiring for the larger rooms. There are good folks around here.

As the boys' father had predicted, or perhaps it was Bonnie, their mother, Peter came back to the shore of Lake Superior. Probably the country's economic storms conspired with his own better nature to bring him home. After catching on with an investment firm in New York, renting an apartment in TriBeCa, and buying a glistening new BMW, he had danced with the lovely daughter of Senator Who, had played tennis with the athletic son of Ambassador Somebody, and had sampled cocaine at strip clubs with Nameless Others.

"We all felt like fried rats in the morning, but pulled on human faces for work, which never began before 10:30 a.m.," he confided to Frederick. "I was stupid. Duluth, the world I knew, seemed too small, and I wanted the world I didn't know instead. Big mistake. I'm not sorry that story fizzled." Frederick touched his brother's shoulder.

Peter had lived the Madoff and found it deadly. Fortunately, he had not risen high enough to be an object of investigation when the facts of his firm's tax evasion and predatory lending, the fleecing of both government and the public, became known. But Peter was damaged goods in the investment community, cracked if not shattered. He'd returned to Duluth that summer to put together the wreckage of his life, which would now be less golden than he'd dreamed when he went East. He landed a job at *RJ Sports* selling motorcycles and snowmobiles, replaced the BMW with last year's Fiesta, and, with his father's help, bought a small house in Piedmont. He kept a gold chain as a memento of his year in the fast lane.

The first time Peter and his father shared a pitcher of Bud at the neighborhood tavern, Ben asked, "So, did you have sex with a Republican?" When he smiled, wrinkles radiated like spokes from the tips of his mouth. I remember his smile well.

"I'm so ashamed," Peter replied. Eavesdroppers assure me that was a yes.

The demand for the products of *Arrowhead Clay* had lessened during the previous year, and so that summer, in the weeks after Frederick's adventure and as Peter pulled himself together, the elder Serafins made the difficult decision to terminate the mining and marketing of clay. The processing and shipping facility was sold, and revenue from the liquidated property was divided between the brothers. The bookstore and the gallery, *Feat of Clay*, remained. As winter approached, the Serafin parents said goodbye to Duluth and moved to Arizona. Since Peter had no interest in bookstores or galleries, the building housing them went to Frederick. Martha kept a low profile as the Serafin family reshaped itself. As I said before, I miss Ben and Bonnie.

Frederick occasionally taught ceramics in the studio behind the gallery, but his own sculpting occupied him more and more. His first success was a life-sized Miranda, built lovingly, his hands shaping the damp clay limb by limb. Sometimes, as a thigh or a breast took shape in his hands, his eyes filled with tears. His Miranda, bare breasted and with a large bird perched on her shoulder, was donated for the lobby of the *Wise Fool Shakespeare* playhouse in Duluth. He sculpted subsequent Mirandas, placing her in various pastoral settings, either with her faun, her leopard, or her unicorn—and always with the rose in her hair.

Some of these, thanks to Martha's publicity efforts, sold quickly. A Miranda with the satyr she'd called Bambi was sold for the library at the University of Wisconsin in Madison, and a Minneapolis philanthropist bought a large installation that included all three of Miranda's outdoor friends together with a tree filled with glass birds of many colors made by Dan Neff, a Duluth glass artist. The installation was donated to the *Guthrie Theatre*. Other pieces in what was now called the Miranda Series remained in storage until a suitable gallery could be found for a major show.

Although she was a frequent volunteer at the homeless shelter, Martha was also a fountain of encouragement in the early days of Frederick's fame, taking on the duties of an agent and the loyalties of a friend. So encouraging had she been about the Miranda Series that when she complimented him on his silk shirt with the stripe on the sleeve—they were in the process of arranging a new show for a local potter that would open the next day at *Feat of Clay*—Frederick attempted to describe his stay at Argo.

"So the shirt was given to you in a dream?" Martha asked, smiling at the story she'd just heard.

"If that's what you want to call it."

"Call it a shirt?"

"No, call it a dream."

Martha's smile turned to worry as she absorbed the odd remark. "So you think that this place called Argo was real?"

"I think reality and dream can mingle." He tried to turn his response into a witticism. "Like rum and Coke, they improve one another."

At the start of the following summer, Frederick decided to buy a house in the hills east of Duluth. The recent collapse in the real estate market would work in his favor as a buyer. Viki and I had lost our own home thanks to deregulation. In any case, teaching ceramics had also ceased to be rewarding for Frederick. Students pestered him about how to hand-build life-sized figures from clay. Were special kinds of clay required? Were interior braces used? One day he caught a young man snooping in his studio, but Frederick was not ready to reveal hard earned secrets, not yet.

The house he found, blue and with a large yard, had a view of the lake through the trees, not unlike the view from Argo. A driveway slanted up the hill to the house, and a flagstone walkway meandered past a cedar tree from the parking site to the house. There were no sculptures by Moore or Giacometti in the yard, but two affordable plaster deer held the white flags of their tails permanently raised. It was an ordinary house, but the location cannot have been far from where Argo had been before its disappearance.

Frederick threw a chain across his driveway, posted No Hunting and No Trespassing signs, and set about building a studio as an addition to the east end of the house. He also added a Jacuzzi and satellite TV. In the lazy warmth of summer, real deer grazed in the yard, joining their plaster likenesses, and an occasional black bear lumbered by. At evening, Frederick sat on his porch, listened to the dark voices of frogs, smelled the air fragrant with the out-of-doors, and wondered what story might be encoded in the flickering of the stars.

He invited Martha to occupy the property in Gary and to manage the bookstore, gallery, and studio there. It would be her business and she would retain all profits, such was the success he'd had. It was a generous offer, but nonetheless ...

"I thought you and I had grown close," she said. After a silence, she invited Frederick to think about his values. "The good life is lived among people, dumbass, not alone on a hill with stones, twigs, and dreams." She had adopted Bonnie Serafin's way of leveling her gaze to serve as an exclamation point. "You'll be lonely. Don't drift way. It can't make you happy." Either from shame or embarrassment, he turned away, leaving her words drifting in the air, words that would live into the future like a ghost in a hallway or a voice in a dream. *The good life is lived among people.*

The new series that absorbed him in his studio up the shore consisted of representations of various people of power and infamy. He often worked in the studio ten hours a day, and after a year the old moving boxes, in slow collapse, still hunkered in corners around the house. To relax, he had placed a bench beneath a maple in the yard where he would sit during gentle rain, gazing up at the underside of leaves and listening to the tapping of the drops.

The first figure was of Bernie Madoff, the sociopath who had stolen the life savings of hundreds of people through his Ponzi scheme, a pitiful man whom no one could pity. Frederick duplicated the man's smile (sociopaths learn charm) and his posture, but a large piece had been removed from the head as though to suggest the absence of whatever gray matter governs sympathy and decency. In another work, Moamar Gadhafi stood erect in military garb, a broken child at his feet. Gadhafi's jaw hung loosely from beneath one ear. A red glaze suggested blood spilling from the gash, and one eye appeared shattered like a child's hammered marble.

Other statues followed, and Frederick called them The Argonauts Series. In the evenings, he read *The Argonautica*, the ancient epic poem by Appollonius Rhodius, which recounted the myth of Jason's quest for the Golden Fleece. But he found the cataloguing tedious—all of the characters listed in the opening pages were enough to turn most modern readers away. He wished he liked the poem more, and it occurred to him that narrative art had come a long way toward finding its own rhythm and its own relationship to human time. The flow of a story, Frederick thought, is so utterly different from the stasis of sculpture. A statue stands outside of time, whereas narrative, like music, is made of time, each day having its syntax and each year with its chapters. Perhaps he'd write a story one day.

But for now, Frederick's static art had a will of its own. It needed to go public. He had replicated two worlds, the pastoral setting of Miranda's arbor by the creek and the nightmare world of the powerful and the greedy imaged by her father—the realm of the rose and the realm of the reptile. Cracked, shattered, or bloody forms now stood in storage beside the Miranda pieces. One day late in September, just as he was shaping the final contours of a head in his studio, his cell phone played its tune. It was Martha, and the news was more than he'd imagined possible.

For years, Garth Clark had owned the country's foremost gallery for ceramic art. The gallery had closed, and he and Mark Del Vecchio had started an exclusively online business. Now they would reopen a brick-and-mortar gallery in the center of New York's Chelsea district, the art collector's American Mecca. Martha's well crafted portfolio had done its job, and Clark & Del Vecchio would begin again in the spring with sculpture by Frederick Serafin.

There was much to do in the intervening months. Garth was committed to finding someone with star quality to author the brochure, and the appropriate publications—*Art Today, The New York Times, The New Yorker*—would receive plenty of advance publicity. Eventually, Jonathan Franzen, the novelist, agreed to meet with Frederick and to consider writing the brochure. Franzen would visit in his home city of St. Louis in November, and to see Franzen there Frederick received from Clark an airline ticket and a hotel reservation.

They met in the Visitors Center at the foot of *The Gateway Arch* that loops along the west bank of the Mississippi River, where, thanks to motorists gazing at the arch just as the interstate executes a horse-shoe bend, the traffic on I-55 South slows to a crawl. For the purpose of ready identification, Franzen arrived in jeans and a maroon and gold University of Minnesota sweatshirt. They spent a few minutes browsing in the *Museum of Westward Expansion*, and then sat over coffee and Frederick's portfolio, which had been sent to Franzen the week before.

"Your publicist has done a great job with this," Franzen said. "Martha Gardner? Isn't that her name?"

"Yes, Gardener, with the extra *e*. She's a good friend."

Franzen's light brown hair fell toward his eyes as he thumbed through the pages, occasionally asking questions. After about 30 minutes he said that he would do the brochure. Frederick's work was a moving testimony to what America and the planet is in the process of losing. The show would be called "Then and Now."

"I'm heartened at the thought of an art exhibit where real-life villains are named," Franzen said. "We live in a culture of pseudo-stories, of perpetual deniability. When he's questioned, the public official says, 'Facts were overlooked.' The passive voice is the veil. *Who* overlooked the facts? The stories about our real world are stories without agents, without protagonists, and so there's no place for the buck to stop. It just keeps circulating. Jesus, we still don't know how JFK was killed. Wouldn't it be wonderful to hear an elected official say, 'I fucked up'? It would be music—*I fucked up.*

"But it's unimaginable today. It makes you appreciate a flood or a hurricane. You know how to direct your response to a natural disaster, where to apply the bulldozers and jackhammers. But we live in a narrative disaster. Anyway, your show reminds us to put real people into our stories about our real world. Of course Americans name the foreign villains you've sculpted. They get named in our stories, but you put them right out there with the Americans hiding behind the passive voice."

"Thanks. Someone should write a book called *The*

Villain with a Thousand Faces," Frederick said. "Anyway, I've had this idea, more a fantasy than an idea, I suppose. But I've imagined the entire collection as being the work of art, not the separate pieces. Everything is relational. There's no such thing as an object or a person in isolation. So each time this collection is shown, I could alter the spacial relationships. People would connect the dots differently each time. Same stars but a different constellation. The relationships would always shift...It would always be a story in progress."

"Like history," Franzen mused.

"But I don't know how such an evolving show could be funded, and I suppose people would lose interest once they get the idea. I get these arty-crappy notions. Anyway, every art opening deconstructs."

"But it's true that in selling off individual pieces the relational aspect is obscured. The destruction of the whole is dictated by market conditions, a comment on our money-driven world. Your show can't survive its own selling. Maybe I can work that into the brochure. I want to visit Duluth for a day or two and see the sculpture first hand. It will also allow me to visit friends in the Twin Cities. My recent novel is set in St. Paul, you may know."

"I'm reading *Freedom*," Frederick replied. "I'm where the story shifts to New York."

"Just to clarify, and this is an overworked distinction, but would you say your sculpture comes from self-expression, or are you up to other things?"

"I'm not interested in self-expression. It would take a fathead to think others should be interested in the little tangle-town inside him. My stuff is about the world out there, not about me."

"Good. I'll telephone about my arrival in Duluth before Thanksgiving, if that works for you."

They concluded their meeting by riding the tram up one side of the arch to the observation area, where they contemplated the river wandering southward below them and beyond it Illinois stretching lazily to the east. In the opposite direction, St. Louis bumped into itself as it sprawled westward, where clouds were mounds of white clay.

*

The burst of autumn color along the shoreline of Lake Superior ended with wind, drizzle, and vanquished leaves spiraling to the ground. The stars that began to appear in a November twilight turned to snow flakes that melted on your face and hair. Soon the lake, which froze over entirely that year as if in answer to the summer's heat, heaved boulders of ice between itself and the land. The ghosts of drowned sailors, said to come up for air from time to time, shivered in forced hibernation until summer. On clear nights, the moon was a bowling ball of ice rolling slowly down its alley above the lake.

Eventually spring arrived with its usual foot-dragging. While other local craftspeople prepared for the Crossing Borders Tour, Frederick and Martha welcomed the arrival of airline tickets to New York and hotel reservations at the *Chelsea Pines,* which was less than ten minutes by cab from the gallery. There may have been some envy in the Duluth art scene, but local artists realized that anything giving Duluth larger lettering on the art map would help them all.

The *vernissage* would be on a Friday evening from 5 to 9 p.m., and Frederick's show would open to the public the following Tuesday, hopefully after rave reviews in the Sunday papers. The Delta flight carrying Frederick and Martha to New York settled down through a thin dusting of clouds almost touching the skyscrapers, as huge, Frederick thought, as the hideous dreams of dictators.

The two Duluthians met Garth Clark and Mark Del Vecchio at the gallery and surveyed the arrangement of the show. The gallery owners were a jovial contrast. Garth, a large man in a sweatshirt, greeted them with a voice that rumbled like a rock slide. Mark, smaller and more buttoned down, spoke in a whisper like breeze over sand.

The gallery consisted of three large show rooms on each of two floors, six rooms in all, as well as a restaurant and a gift shop. The show-room décor was subdued so as not to compete with the art, while the gift shop and restaurant were elaborate improvisations of color and form worthy of a film set for "Avatar."

"Then and Now" occupied the first floor, and the Miranda and Argonaut pieces were interspersed rather than arranged as separate groups. In one instance, the raised head of a faun appeared to gaze in shock at Bernie Madoff. In another, Miranda lay at the feet of Syria's murderous dictator, Bashar al-Assad, whose last name means "the lion," a nice irony in view of Miranda's peaceable outdoor friends. Frederick approved of the arrangement and was delighted by the storyboards containing text from Franzen's brochure.

One board, placed beside the largest Miranda installation, offered an informative paragraph on the pastoral tradition by which, throughout the ages, poets and artists have used rural settings as a position from which to critique the larger world. Another storyboard contextualized the Argonaut pieces with a discussion of our own post-9/11 world of tyranny, greed, and violence. A third praised Serafin's theatrical imagination, revealed in his ability to capture telling gestures within a symbolic space.

For Frederick and Martha, the afternoon of the opening consisted of unnecessary agonizing over what to wear, which was finally quieted via the semi-formal compromise. Frederick slipped into a camel hair jacket over an open collar, while Martha chose black slacks and a blue silk blouse.

The dress of the patrons that evening ran the gamut. All eyes stole glances at a woman of at least six feet tall who wore an evening gown revealing the glistening flesh of her back, which seemed sculpted of the finest ivory. Her petite friend, on the other hand, wore blue jeans and a black Honey Badger tee stretched tight across acorn nipples. A short man, who was whispered to be Donald Trump's buyer—"The Donald is building something again," Mark confided—wore a standard-issue dark suit, thick glasses, and a beard like the tail-feathers of a mallard. Steve Martin, in sweater and slacks, sipped Champaign from a flute, and Angelina Jolie, in town to promote a film on *The Daily Show*, charmed the room in her peasant skirt. Mark also pointed out reviewers from *The New Yorker* and *The Times*.

Frederick was disturbed by how the scene reminded him of the Glass Room at Argo, with all of the transitioning manikins frozen in mid-sentence. Was he now in a world any less artificial?

He had determined to remain in the background as visitors circulated, speaking if spoken to but not putting himself forward. An opening is about the art, not the artist. Also, it can be disconcerting to hear people's unguarded thoughts about one's work. Nonetheless, he overheard a man remark that the most profound aspect of his own experience with art is the wide chasm between the claims made for the art by others and his own evaluation of it. It was the mystery of that gap that intrigued him. "When I contemplate art, I'm like a scientist exploring the vacuum," he concluded. Frederick feared that this man might be the only honest person in the room.

On the other hand, Angelina Jolie spoke to Frederick briefly, assuring him that she would try to place one of his Argonaut pieces where it could be viewed by the public in Los Angeles. She promised to start by talking to friends at *The L.A. County Museum*. Steve Martin said a brief hello, but it wasn't clear what he thought of the show.

A youngish man with blond hair and coal-black eyes caught Frederick's attention. The man's pale skin nearly matched the bleached white of the Argonauts, and he lacked a right hand. A glass lizard hung from a neck chain. It was curious to watch him circulate among representations of moral damage, almost as though he were part of the show. He was not Preston Morgan but, Frederick thought, almost certainly a relative, and more than once Frederick stifled the urge to approach him. Meanwhile, Martha had been cornered at the bar by a handsome black man in a gray business suit who probably had romance in mind.

The rooms were filled from 5 to 9, as cases of Champaign emptied. One inebriate in sneakers and shorts nearly stumbled into the installation depicting Richard Fuld, past CEO of *Lehman Brothers,* sneaking stealthily from the LB Building. When the financial firm collapsed, Fuld had made off with 345 million, a fleecing that earned him his place among the Argonauts.

But no harm was done by the drunk, and as the crowd thinned the glow of success hung in the air. Clark and Del Vecchio stayed another hour to attend to security issues and paper work, and Frederick and Martha had a nightcap at the hotel and then a few more, after which they found themselves, or lost themselves, in Martha's bed.

In the morning, Frederick awoke with his nerves crackling like downed power lines. He rolled himself over carefully, met Martha's gazed, and asked, "Did we . . ?"

"I think so," she replied, stretching, rolling from the bed, and executing a mock stomp to the bathroom. Apparently all of the hangover had landed like debris from the sky on Frederick.

When she returned, a towel turbaned about her

head and her caramel skin glistening, Frederick muttered, "And so did we use . . ?"

"I know I didn't," she said. "Can you buy morning-after pills in New York?"

"Plan B? I'll call room service," he declared, rising to the occasion, stumbling to the phone, and stubbing a toe on the leg of a chair.

Later, properly fed and caffeinated, they spent an hour on the spiraling floors of the *Guggenheim* before catching a Saturday afternoon flight to Minneapolis, which baked in another greenhouse-gassed summer, and an evening hop to Duluth, only slightly cooler by the lake. They dozed fitfully through both flights.

*

On the following Thursday, Frederick sat on his porch reading *Maggie's American Dream,* a book that Martha had mentioned about an African-American family. He paused from time to time to pluck an apple from a basket and toss it to a deer in the yard. Eventually, he received a call on his cell phone from Martha.

"A lot of pretty good news from Garth and some a little bit iffy. Wanna wash the clay off and drive in for lunch?"

He'd had nothing to do with clay that morning and therefore was in Gary in forty minutes. They drove to *Hulda's House,* a small restaurant half way up the hill, where, I'm proud to say, everything is served on dinner ware made by my wife—those connections again. Frederick and Martha took a table on the patio that offered them a partial view of the estuary. A fishing boat nodded gently in the distance, and beyond it the clouds on the Wisconsin shore shifted slowly. Down the shore to the east, a freighter approached the Aerial-Lift Bridge to enter the harbor. The crows in a nearby maple erupted in a chorus of caws.

"It's a caw-cus," Martha said.

"Sounds to me like *Hardball* with Chris Mathews," Frederick offered.

"Yeah, that gets hard to listen to sometimes. Anyway, how's your brother doing?" Martha asked.

"I'm proud of Peter. He's tired of selling mopeds and wants to find a more useful life, and he met a girl on the Internet. I think she lives in Colombo.

"Sri Lanka? How in the world did their threads cross?" Martha asked.

"One of those dating sites. It's run out of India."

"Out-sourcing love," Martha mused. "I wonder how that works."

"You get a list of names and start playing cyberfootsie."

"Cybernibbles?"

"Cyber...never mind. Anyway, she flies to the states in a month." The waitress arrived, and they ordered salads.

"Maybe Peter would like to pitch in at the Mission," Martha suggested. She was now a regular volunteer. "He admires you, you know. He stopped in at *Feat of Clay* the other day and talked about how you learn by using your imagination, whereas a 'doofus' like him—his word—has to learn the hard way. But he's smart. He remarked on people for whom money has none of the usual uses. It isn't about buying or security. It's just about itself. 'These people acquire billions just to have billions,' he said, 'billions they don't ever literally touch. These guys live in a reality that's just numbers.' His critique was interesting. Peter's on our side now."

"I'm proud of him. I'll mention the Mission. Good idea, kiddo."

"By the way, he asked me who Miranda is...or was."

"And you said?"

"I said Miranda is what you call your muse."

"Good. Thank you."

"And Bonnie and Ben? Are your folks overheating in Arizona?"

"Mom's other knee will be replaced, so she's unhappy. Dad is doing better...playing a little golf on cooler mornings. They drive around taking in scenery."

"Sand? Cactus?"

"Old Native American villages and state parks."

"Strange how nomadic even retired people are in America," Martha said. "Yearning is an American malady. Anyway, Garth called. Your work is selling. Financially, the *vernissage* was a huge success—one of the best openings he's ever had. He's a little bit miffed that you didn't tell him about the Argonauts—the real ones. He reminded me that real people and organizations can decide to sue, and using their names needs to be mulled over carefully." She examined Frederick's face. "I remember you talked about Argonauts after that kayak accident a couple years ago. Is this related?"

I think Martha had come to believe Frederick had experienced something real during the Flood of 2012. Let's just say that she had.

"After the accident," Frederick said, "I...thought I'd met someone who talked about a group of businessmen with that name. But then maybe I'd just had my marbles rearranged. It was like I'd landed in one of those interactive computer games where you take an active role in a fictional world. It was weird. I didn't hear of that group again, so I didn't think much about using the name. Anyway, the word Argonaut is public property, isn't it?"

"Well, Garth said that too. Also, *Argo Enterprises* has purchased some of your pieces. He doesn't think someone would begin a law suit with a large purchase. But you never know."

"*Argo Enterprises*? Jesus. I had no idea."

"And Donald Trump bought the Bernie Madoff. Garth joked that it was probably hero worship, so his mood isn't in bad shape. Oh, and someone bought the Richard Fuld, and Garth thinks the buyer is Fuld's rep. They probably have more money than God."

"They're buying my stuff to keep it out of sight, to break up the show. It's divide and conquer. I didn't create these things to have them hidden away." A tourist boat moved slowly across the harbor.

"Maybe you've been quid-pro-quoed," Martha said, poking at the salad that had just arrived, "but couldn't it be they just like your stuff? Anyway, people will see your work the usual way...in magazines and books. Pictures of all your pieces were in Franzen's brochure, and it's available online. Garth says there will be a major article with photos in *Art in America*. And so on."

"The Argonauts don't have a serious thought in their heads." Frederick continued to brood over his surprise buyers. "They're like a college fraternity with their secret handshakes, only they amuse themselves by messing with the world. And they buy up the protest. It isn't what I had in mind in creating the show."

"Don't go all conspiracy theory on me. The world improves with time. Look at the Great Migration and the Freedom Rides. At their worst, the guys you talk about are the undertow. The ship goes forward," Martha said. "Anyway, art is a crazy market. You can't price things to be affordable to the average Joe or Jane. No big-time gallery could touch it. No magazine would review it. The high price is part of the attraction. You can sell something for $100,000 easier than for $10,000. But rich people usually end up loaning or donating to museums. It's a matter of pride. I wouldn't worry. Plus, I'm getting my period."

"Rockin' good news! So we don't have to get married or call Planned Parenthood?"

"No one has to get married these days, dumb-dumb. You need to get out more."

He smiled, remembering the day she had talked about the Great Migration as they sat on the porch of

Feat of Clay. Her words back then had gotten him out into a world he had not thought much about, and he had read about the Migration in *The Warmth of Other Suns*. Also, he remembered how she had asked him to be careful not to harm the ants. Today her cheeks had the same glow, as if transmitting an inner light.

"Wanna get married anyway?" he asked. An elderly couple at a neighboring table looked on.

She lowered her head and gave him the emphatic look. "Two kids or three?"

"Whatever you say, darling."

"Wow! No assembly required!" The couple next-door laughed aloud. "But you gotta work on your sugar talk, white man."

"Is that a yes?" He watched the boat nodding in the estuary. The crows in Hulda's trees continued their endless debates.

"Yes, it's a yes."

"And all along I figured that black guy in the suit at the *vernissage* had the inside track."

"Lawrence Whodat? He said he'd love me eight days a week, and there was something about the wine of my eyes and the dark radiance of my skin. Now that's sugar-talk, Fred. But when I tried to make him settle for five days a week, he lost interest."

"Good. I'll make rings of clay then."

"Hey bro, my Great-Granny Indiana didn't leave Monroe for no ring of clay. You been turnin' clay to gold, and this black girl wants the gold." And then, becoming her newer self again, she mentioned a line she remembered from *The Tempest*, "Journeys end with lovers meeting."

"And then new journeys begin," Frederick said.

The couple at the next table stood to leave, smiling and wishing Frederick and Martha well. The fishing boat in the estuary nodded in agreement, while on the Wisconsin side clouds continued their slow transformations. A gull turned on spread wings like a small craft coming about on water.

"Are you finished floating," Martha asked, "or just docked for repairs."

"The floating life is over." *Everything changes,* Frederick thought, and Martha did too. Proteus had been working overtime. As they walked back to the car, Martha noticed the writing on the side of a small church nearby: *The Lord is My Journey.* Clouds were painted above the slogan.

"Another journey," Martha mused. "It's a wonder you can find anyone at home these days."

"Our scudding lives," he said. The déjà-vu moment passed.

That afternoon Frederick accompanied Martha to the Mission, where he participated in clean-up efforts in the dining area and in the sleeping area upstairs. In the hallway upstairs, an old man emerged slowly from a bathroom. The remains of his hair were ponytailed Willie Nelson style, and he was shirtless. His arms dangled beside a ribcage that was like an ancient washboard, and his face had been bashed. The iris of one eye seemed immersed in a pulp of egg white and blood. A sound dropped from his mouth as he turned and limped away down the hall.

Downstairs, a small room for socializing contained a scuffed carpet with a long obliterated design and an old, box TV with a scratched and dusty screen. A dark-skinned woman, motionless on an old sofa, gazed at the screen with glassy eyes as she picked at dead skin by a finger nail. The TV was off, and it was as if her mind had collapsed inward.

A mind can be like a garden, Frederick thought, but also like a tomb. Nothing was attractive in the Mission. He glanced back at the woman picking at herself, her eyes still fixed on the empty screen. Who would choose such scenery? Behind her, a wasp buzzed against a window pane. Frederick remembered the room at Argo that had seemed to breathe sunlight and then Miranda's conversation about the mind being a garden with "borrowed scenery." Here, time hung in the air like dust.

Later, Martha explained that the woman had car-cooked her baby while drinking an afternoon away in the *Twins Bar.* She had just been released from two years of jail/rehab. "I don't think that woman will make it," Martha said, her Milky Way smile obscured by cloud cover. "When you get her talking, she tells you her daughter is visiting Grandma, and she really believes it. We all need our stories, but ..."

"Yeah," Frederick said. "I remember seeing my grandmother dying in the nursing home, her memories becoming more odd with each day. She was like collapsed clay on a wheel."

For the near future, Frederick would fill his life by financing renovations and improvements at *Safe Harbor Mission*, and Peter's financial skills might make him a star on the team. There was space enough in the building to add a small library where classes could be taught, perhaps classes in life skills such as how to apply for a job and keep a personal budget—or whatever else the social workers might advocate. And Frederick could build a studio where people could learn ceramics. If the Argonauts intended to buy up his sculpture, he would at least use the money constructively. Recalling that first morning at Argo and the words of Dr. Graves, whose small eyes sparkled between bulging sideburns, Frederick realized that now he would "recycle" himself.

At 5:00 o'clock the dining room filled with a shuffling cross-section of homelessness—tired old men muttering to the air—dazed bag ladies in their middle years—and young people, black, white, Latino, and Native American, each with eyes like lost islands. The room smelled of liver and onions. Frederick studied one table at which about a dozen of the homeless sat.

One could do a sculpture, he thought, on the model of Leonardo's "Last Supper." The clay figures could be placed at a real wooden table set with real plates. The center position at the table, occupied by Jesus in the painting, would be empty. It could be a commentary on our world's lost center. But no, he was done with sculpture and installations. It was time to work with real people. He remembered Martha's words about the good life.

The doorway to the street was blocked by an old man contorting into a jacket a size too small. He muttered as Frederick and Martha slipped by. As they walked back to their car, a city bus, grunting and panting, stopped at the corner to allow an old lady to pick her way slowly down the steps and onto the sidewalk, where she did a stutter step to regain balance. Her gray hair was frayed and random, a hacked-at look. She turned in the direction of *Safe Harbor*.

"So," Frederick said as he dropped Martha back at *Feat of Clay*, "if we're doing this marriage thing, do you want to live out on the hill or here in town? I'd like to come back to town."

"Come back, bro, by all means. We need to get you a social life, and you'll have *Safe Harbor* now."

Later that evening he wondered at the strangeness of the return of so many memories of Argo that afternoon—the wasp in the window, the mind as a garden. The following morning he called a real estate agent, and then he sorted through his possessions, separating the *Good Will* donations from the keepers. The agent arrived at ten, a perky young woman from *Edina Realty*. She had scarcely passed through the door when she tried to say how thrilled she was to meet such a great artist.

"How did you hear about what I do?" he asked.

"The *Duluth News Tribune* had a big write-up on your opening in New York. You didn't know? It was on the same page as a report on the high suicide rate among victims of predatory lending and foreclosures. It really underlined your theme. *Edina* only sells to people who can afford it, by the way."

Then, after glancing around at the mess, she observed with a coy smile that he must spend all of his time sculpting. "We need to do a lot of cleaning and some renovation. And you need air conditioning," she said, mopping a brow. "For every $100 spent preparing the house you'll get back three."

"This isn't really about the money," Frederick said. "I just want to get it sold."

"Moving to New York?"

"No, the scale of things is hideous there. I'm joining the home team again."

"The house will sell faster if you make a few improvements. You can always accept a low-ball offer if you're in a hurry. What say I get a contractor out here tomorrow? I'll come too. I have contract forms so we can put everything in writing. You need things on paper when you're dealing with contractors, even in friendly old Duluth."

That afternoon, realizing that there was another renovation to be done, he phoned an architect concerning the Mission. Then he drove a pickup truck loaded with books, utensils, clothing, and furniture all piled together like football players going for a fumble. His destination was the *Good Will* on Garfield Avenue. He knew that some of the stuff might be used at *Safe Harbor*, but he had decided that everything he brought there would be new.

Returning to the house up the shore, as a crow eyed him from a branch over his driveway, he found a small package in his mail box by the county road. He opened it while sitting on his porch in the deep green of summer while a doe and her new faun grazed the lawn and browsed the trees. Inside the package was a small, glass unicorn and a note.

Dear Frederick,

This unicorn was made from Miranda, who transitioned after sustaining injuries in a storm at sea in the Mediterranean. Most of us escaped when we ran aground on an island, but Miranda was injured and then a fever set in. Dr. Graves thought that lack of contact with the larger world may have weakened her immune system. It was her last, barely audible wish that you have something of her.

Personally, I want to congratulate you on your recent show, but I'll also mention that Father wasn't pleased. His words were, "Whatever story he thinks he's telling, I intend to counter it." You happen, I suppose inadvertently, to have represented a few of his colleagues in your sculptures. I calmed him down, and he opted just to buy a few of the pieces to diminish unfavorable publicity for Argo Enterprises. So I need to tell you, for instance, that once the show closes the world will never see your Richard Fuld again. It's dirty business, but your price was paid.

Dad's transitioning had an extended remission after you left Argo, but it's moving rapidly now. Soon his wing of the Argonauts will fall to me. I'll fight for changes in the Argonaut philosophy, but there will be plenty of opposition—a mess I don't look forward to. Perhaps the global-warming crisis, now acknowledged even by Dad's crowd, will help facilitate change.

We travel through life erasing and rewriting ourselves like movie characters with dark glasses, aliases, and a box of passports.

Sadly,

Preston Morgan
Your Brother in Another Life

It was a message and a gift that had crossed many borders. The unicorn was formed of different colors of melted glass. An external layer was transparent, and within the body veins of red, blue and purple swirled and flowed as if alive. The horn was small, like the horn on the faun in Miranda's arbor. Frederick stared into the glass figure for a long while as shadows crept across the lawn, eventually chasing the living deer into the trees as twilight darkened and tumbled into evening, leaving the ornamental deer to stand guard through the night.

In the last light, the moon was a ghostly ship wrecked on an island of cloud. Then Frederick gazed beyond it into our corner of the universe, contemplating the constellations. A meteor fell, a thread pulled from another world and blazing out. Insects whispered in the grass.

Miranda's revels had ended even as he had turned to new ones. As for the piece of her that Preston had sent, it would live as an inconspicuous mystery among other art objects in his collection. Perhaps he had a tear or two to brush away—yes, let us say that there were tears. Miranda would be a memory that would rise and fall in his mind, like something lost at sea. He would dream sometimes, as raindrops whispered on a roof, of a strange ship leaving a harbor with a girl in white on its deck, a rose in her hair. But the dreams, too, would slip away with the passing years. He will have become another person.

For now, there would be Martha Gardener, a name

he hoped she would keep, and the *Safe Harbor Mission*. Work needed doing, he thought, work with people not with mud. It would be a busy summer, beginning next week when Peter would join in meeting with the architect at the Mission. Frederick, with Martha's help and with his brother's as well, intended to be happy and useful. A good life is lived among people, and Martha had taught him that we are defined by the quality of our relationships with others. The arts, he thought, can be a way of creating relationships, but they are not ends in themselves.

He slept well that night as a passing rain whispered for a while in the trees, and then the morning came fresh and clean along the lake.

STORIES

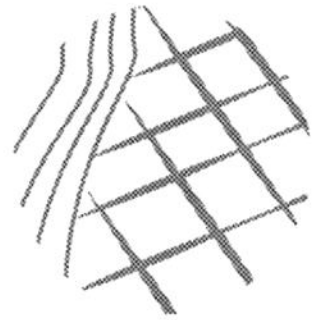

Rejection

It was on the scenic route north of Hinckley. I'd pulled into this one-pump country store for gas, but then the engine wouldn't start. Sometimes it just needed a rest...time to cool down. Karin used to say it was chillin'. But it's no fun taking a whiz out in the middle of the scenery and then your car won't start. It's unsettling.

I decided to take a walk, so I went back in the store and bought a Snickers. There was this picnic table about half a mile down the road with a trash barrel filled to the top. A crow on the rim tossed bags and wrappers around, trying to pig out. Or crow out. Whatever. Autumn leaves on the ground were like pieces of a jigsaw puzzle, and the table was chained to cement in the ground. Everyone's chaining their stuff down these days.

I hoisted myself onto the table and put my feet on the bench, avoiding the bird shit with my butt. Across the road was this cross nailed to a tree. Branches above the cross came together like when you fold your hands, like the trees were religious or something. Behind the trees a couple of cows poked around in a field. One of them looked up and stared at me like I was something suspicious. The lookout cow. I tore the wrapper on the Snickers, but then decided to save it for later. I walked over to check out the cross. There were flowers and a handwritten sign stuck in the ground beside the cross.

In Loving Memory
Rhonda, Age 11
May, 2010

I went back to sit on the table and think about Karin. I probably looked like that statue of the man thinking, only he was naked. Anyway, me and Karin had been together three years. Pendulum years, I called them. On the up side of the arc, Karin would sober up. We'd throw out the empties and clean the ash trays. She'd get a pen and a pad of paper, and we'd make plans, her pen tapping as we talked.

In those periods, she was all crucifixes and rosaries. We'd go to mass, she'd say, and God would help. Maybe He'd help us open that bike shop we'd talked about. Karin could fix a bike like no one else. Or maybe we'd get the farm house we always wanted and even have a kid. In those days, she thought everything would be fine if you just tossed out the empties and made plans. If you just had faith, each day would be progress.

But the cleaned up days never lasted. When I said that once, she yelled at me for going down that road. She said I was all dark roads and bad weather. I said that life is just another kind of weather, that we don't live intended lives. So we had issues. Everyone has "issues" these days, even when it's just the same old trashcan of drunkenness, lies, and the rent you can't pay. So the pendulum always swung the other way.

Later, back in our apartment, her white bathrobe might slip to the floor like snow from a branch. Or maybe we'd drink quietly on the porch and watch the evening rise like water between houses and down the street. And there was this bar with a juke box where she taught me to dance. Weekends were country-western, all boots and heels and Hank on the juke, but Wednesday was tango night. Karin had legs up to Canada. I loved the tango, especially the slow parts with the bandoneon and violin yearning.

Then we'd sit in a corner booth and talk about the bars in Buenos Aires a hundred years ago, when the tango was born among sailors and prostitutes. We'd try to imagine their lonely lives, the violence and longing of the men on shore and of the women in the dark brothels. Karin's thoughts flared like matches in the dim light. She said that abandoned things have their own special beauty. The bar was our place to dream, and we became different people there.

Other nights she'd stumble off alone, yelling after a fight, and later, with everything adrift, I'd wander off too, wander off and wake up the next morning with someone whose name I'd forgotten. Wake up hearing rain on a strange roof and watching the darkness leak away, leaving the morning behind like something drowned. Eventually, me and Karin would find our separate ways home, maybe with a blade of early light slicing through the trees and under the shade in the kitchen. She'd make coffee, and we'd whisper a few words—"You okay?"—"Yeah, I'll survive."

Even on the worst days, when the old ways pulled us back like quicksand, I wanted Karin. Love is fire, but I can't describe it. Karin was like the weather, like wind that tears itself apart until it's only scraps of wind here and there.

And Pete, Karin's dad, would come around with his face like a headlight shouting about how I was ruining his daughter's life. He was wide as a Ford, and his cheeks hung below his jaw like tar melting. I said I loved Karin, but he said I wasn't talking English. He said if I loved her I'd get a job, and then he'd always bring up how I'd been in jail. He had a black belt in resentment. Me and this other guy had taken a trip to Texas and bought a boat and went to Mexico for weed. I can't swim, but I figured what the hell.

To hear Pete, you'd think we were the effing Taliban. Pete believed something like that, believed we were working for some foreign government. He was a conspiracy nut, inventing plots 24/7. "I'm connecting the dots," he'd say. It was like he was inventing constellations only not in the sky. One day, with Karin yelling her face off, I chased Pete's fat ass away with my gun.

Our tango days were gone, and sunrise was always

a slap in the face. After that I left. This guy I knew said he knew someone at an auto dealership in Two Harbors and maybe I could get a job there. I doubted it, but I went anyway. In those days, Karin spent her time yelling at politicians on the Capital steps in St. Paul and banging drums at the screw-you fat cats in the lobby of the *IDS Building* in Minneapolis. She thought she could fix the universe by hanging around banging drums.

"You can't just run away to the end of the world," she said. "You gotta do more than just have dreams. You gotta move forward." So she'd changed. More weather. Sometimes I preferred her drunk. Anyway, she didn't want any taste of Two Harbors. I left in the old blue Chevy with the starting issues. I'd bought it for both of us, Karin and me. It had some rust, so the price was good.

So I sat there on that picnic table by the bird shit with my fist under my chin like in that statue, except that I had my clothes on and was munching my Snickers. The crow was on the trash barrel, and I identified. A crow on a trash barrel by someone else's picnic table. That's me too. Across the road, that same cow was looking at me while the other one munched grass. Suspicious cow and hungry cow. Pretty soon they'd haul their milk bags back to the barn and evening would flow in like water.

It was time to wonder if the Chevy would start. You don't want to be out on a strange road at night in a car that won't start. You want to be in a bar someplace, or a motel. Maybe I'd stop in Duluth, where I knew a good bar. I wasn't far from Duluth.

I tossed the candy wrapper to my buddy on the trash barrel. Maybe in a couple of minutes I'd toss out the empty knocking around under the car seat. The cross by the pasture was in shadows now, and darkness drained out of the tangled trees above the cross, out of the folded hands. I thought how the sign at the cross might as well say Stanley and Karin, but it didn't. It said Rhonda.

This first section has the structure of a complete story. You present a character in a situation, you extricate him from the situation, and you allow him a moment of insight or epiphany at the end. I especially like the way Stanley's epiphany is associated with a cross, reminding us of the religious origin of the word. And you do it economically and with a certainly lyrical evocation of the lives and frustrations of your characters. Good stuff.

Two

Karin, when you and I were young and things were bad, I'd sit in *Ned's Nasty Secret* in Minneapolis and remember my father, who was in the grave by then but always there in my memory's crawl spaces too, reaching to pull me back. Mom and I lived in a trailer by an alley, and Dad slouched in various dingy bars clutching a bottle next to ash trays and match books, clutching it like you'd grab a utility pole in a hurricane. At least that's how I thought of it. I always wanted to know my dad and have him know me, but it never happened.

As I nursed my own bottle in the *Nasty Secret,* fantasies drifting, I'd imagine flying back in time to search Dad's old haunts on the skids of Washington Avenue. Maybe it would be late on a Saturday afternoon in 1960, one of those October days when homeless men worry about winter as scraps tumble along the street mirroring the swift high clouds. The men gather in doorways to talk of freight trains and journeys, their underground language punctuated by the squeak of corks in bottles, their arms moving for warmth like damaged wings.

In this fantasy, my father and I huddle in an old wooden booth by a window that frames a neon sign. The booth is a mausoleum, its surfaces etched with cigarette burns and carved with names and dates that ripple like a river beneath the touch. We feel the lonely beauty of time passing in derelict places, of various lives weaving together to form a story, a history. Outside, beyond the dusty window, the sky grows dark as any sea. Perhaps the clouds separate from time to time to reveal the ancient starlight, the worlds beyond worlds and the layers of time beyond need.

In the orange glow of the neon, I sit across the scarred table from my father. On the juke, Billy Eckstine sings Ellington's "Solitude." It's as though I'm home. I buy my father a beer and crack the cellophane on a pack of Luckies. We talk in low voices, slowly releasing the past from its silence.

I ask him if the drinking life began for him, as it did for me, with the thrill of sex lacing the smoke of jazz clubs and pool halls. Contemplative behind his cigarette, matching his words to the currents of longing drinkers ride, he tells his story. As the neon whispers and flickers, we drink, taken by absence and desire, our bodies at rest in the void, our lives turning away from the world like motes in a shaft of sunlight. We carve our names.

But I don't think about my father much anymore. Today, I stood by the lighthouse on the shore of Lake Superior in Two Harbors and flung stones sidearm out onto the water. Barbara, my new friend, was with me, tossing stones too. The stones skipped a few times and sunk, and the surface was still again. The ending of a story is a stone sinking into the unsaid.

I fail to understand why you introduce this digression on the father. It does play off of the narrator's frustration with Karin's father, but if we are to relate his rejecting Karin with some residual issue concerning his own father—well, it just isn't clear. You introduce a story element here that needs much more elaboration. Moreover, you end this section (as you ended the first) with a scene and an observation that we'd expect to find at the end of the entire story. But you opt to go on, as though you don't really believe in the moments you've dramatized. Maybe I'm just having a bad day, but there's something here that just doesn't answer to my notions of what a story should be.

Three

On good evenings in Minneapolis, evenings when we weren't fighting, we'd step out the front door, avoid the hole in the porch, walk down the rotting steps, and wander over to *Ned's Nasty Secret* on Franklin Avenue. It had a backroom with a juke box where Karin taught me to dance. I loved the strut and glide of the tango, and I loved holding Karin during the slow parts as the bandoneon yearned.

The notion of just leaving her blew in like a storm. I suppose we dumped each other. Anyhow, I live in Two Harbors now. It's cold here, and the winter wind hits hard. On calm summer days, the lake and the sky are like pages in a book where the ink has vanished, pages that meet at the Wisconsin shoreline. On windy days, the waves and clouds are writing in a foreign language. My life is like a story in a language I can't read. It's been two years. I got that job at *Sonju Motors* and sold a Fiesta and a Fusion last week, so there's some money now.

My new friend, Barbara, likes to fish. We do that together, then I clean and she cooks. We live in an old house her dad left her. I suppose she's my second harbor. She's pregnant so we might get married, but it's no big deal. I wonder if Karin thinks about me and how I took the car. It's probably a story she told for months. I'm probably a character in a story that stopped being told.

Dreams glimmer away, and time waits by the road with a knife. Our lives aren't intended things, not a straight road to the next town. We had dreamed, Karin and me, that we'd live at the edge of a quiet town and raise horses. We'd have a place like one we'd seen from a highway once, a house with a solid roof and a yard with cedar trees and a maple. There would be a pond reflecting clouds and sky, and we'd have a dog...and maybe a kid.

In the late afternoon we'd sit on the porch and see, far away, an abandoned barn sinking into the rippling grass like a battered ship. In autumn there would be geese in wedges inching their way south across the sky. We'd sip beer on the porch and talk about Buenos Aires, about the sailors and the tango and about going there one day, following the geese. Or maybe following a hawk high up, arcing with bowed wings as though travelling invisible curves in space. Then, as the evening climbed the hills and the trees exhaled insects, the grass and barn and hawk would dissolve in a gray wash.

That was our dream. I used to think that you had to hold on to your dreams, that compromising your dreams meant failure. Now I'm not sure. Mostly I go to work. I try to help Barbara be happy, and I'm happy too when we lie together and I feel her whispered breath. But once is forever, and I still imagine the road that passed the home Karin and I had longed for, the road that led away as darkness gathered.

By the end of the second part, you've given the narrator a new life and you've let the stone (story?) sink. But then you reject that ending, haul the stone to the surface, and throw poor Stanley back into his past with Karin. You even repeat the scene in the bar with the tango! Please understand that I'm not trying to tell you what your story should be about, just that it needs to ***be*** *a story.*

You violate the forward trajectory that we expect from a story. We expect an arrow, but you toss us a boomerang. I'm sorry, but there's just something messy here. Good luck with your writing, and please keep BFR in mind in the future.

Walter Smith, Editor-in-Chief

Big Fish Review

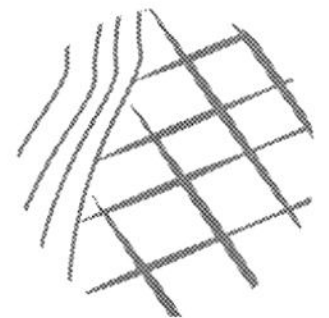

Laura, in the Misty Light

L*aura* was only half ghost. She didn't sigh, moan, or rattle chains in a cellar, and she didn't hang out in some dreary cemetery. She wanted love. Love was her unfinished project, and it took her everywhere. Half ghost and half muse, she drifted in the world of poetry and music, of art and adventure. She haunted me for a time.

She was the Laura that Petrarch saw in the Church of Sainte-Claire in Avignon centuries ago. She told me the story on our first night together. It was raining.

"He was there because the papacy moved to Avignon for most of the 14th century," she explained. "I hardly knew him, but Petrarch didn't care. He had just given up on being a priest, and his hormones were flowing. To him, I was like the girl from Ipanema, only he didn't just sit back and sigh. He was a honey badger. It took threats, but he finally got the message and left me alone. A few years later I heard about his poems to Laura. They made him famous, but it creeped me out...like love letters from Ted Bundy. After I died I became a ghost, but Petrarch had nothing to do with that. I certainly didn't return to look for him!"

"And you've been a ghost ever since?"

"Well, yeah. You don't change back, silly."

On another occasion she told me about her brief affair with Johnny Mercer, who wrote a song about her "face in the misty light."

"Johnny didn't know I was a ghost. We just hung out for a while in Savannah. When I bailed on him, he wrote the song. Like Petrarch, sort of."

I suppose in her more than seven-hundred years of ghosting and musing, I'm not the only nobody she crossed paths with. Even though I had writing aspirations, I'm not comparing myself with the poets and musicians she'd known. She and I were together for a few months, when I was an MFA candidate at the university in Duluth.

It was that final, hanging-around stage. I just needed to finish a collection of stories, and I'd be a rubber-stamped writer. My fiction concerned the counter-culture of the 1960's, when my parents were kids. I was a history major as an undergrad, and that interest obviously influenced my writing. As a grad student, I'd been allowed to earn chump change teaching metallically ornamented undergraduates about your plots and your characters, your conflicts and your closure. Not to mention your commas and your semicolons.

Laura sat in the front row, often fingering the scar that ran from a swirl of brown hair to the middle of her cheek. During the third week, she materialized on a stool next to mine clutching a bouquet of poems and drawings. The setting was *The Burger Hub* in the Kirby Student Center, where a candy-colored juke box, a sparkling replica of the music boxes of a gone era, played "Summer in the City."

"I need to know if these are any good. I mean, in your opinion."

They were spectacularly good, evoking yearnings and mysteries in their descriptions of far-flung cities and landscapes. Who was I to teach her? But I wanted to know her. When summer arrived, she and I shared a cabin that commanded a half-acre lot sloping down to Island Lake. It belonged to Lawrence, my upward-mobile brother, and was on loan to me while he and his new wife, Barbara Stevenson of *Stevenson Enterprises*, ambled the summer away in Provence and Tuscany. He'd met Barbara in a boss-and-secretary bar near the *IDS Building* in Minneapolis, and they were married within five months. While they popped corks in Isle-sur-la-Sorgue or hiked trails in the Luberon, I was Allen the Cabin Sitter.

I was also the black sheep of the family, lagging well behind my entrepreneurial siblings. For me, the common instruction manual for navigating life's rapids offered too many ways to drown. There'd be no ordinary life for me. I would exist above or beyond the routines of normalcy. Life, I thought, should be a series of magical moments, stepping stones across the rapids.

I'd decided that the best way to pursue these moments was to be a writer, a calling that would open the gates of the higher world. Lawrence's cabin would be the place for my journey to begin, and Laura's presence would add to the magic. She'd be my muse. So there we were, Laura and I, paddling the lake in Lawrence's canoe, barbecuing in Lawrence's pit, building fires in Lawrence's fireplace on chill nights, and sporting us like amorous birds of prey in Lawrence's bed. It didn't occur to me that the pursuit of my dreams was financed by my brother's real-world labors.

Two

Laura had come to Duluth from New Orleans, where she had drifted about in the wake of Katrina. With dark hair and eyes, she had adopted a Cajun persona, accent and all. I called her "sha" and "cher," the extent of my own knowledge of the Cajun lingo, and I imagined her dancing barefoot by a Louisiana bayou in the setting sun, her hair flying in rhythm with a nearby fiddle.

As my story collection transformed itself into an incipient novel in the circuits of my laptop that summer at Island Lake, I learned that Laura also had an intriguing cast of fictional friends, along with a real cat. Sometimes after a late-night walk, she'd return with her lantern, her hair wilded by the wind, and claim to have been with other ghosts of long-gone writers—Virginia Wolfe, perhaps, or Rilke.

"They're ghosts too now," she explained. "It's a network. Ghosts are part of the world's fabric, you know, even though you don't always see us."

At night she prayed to sprites and fairies. "They're very small, and they live inside of flowers. They have little sparks inside of them, so they glow...sort of. They're comforting, but they don't really help much."

Another person, not a ghost, whom she visited on her walks was Katiana. Laura described her as an elderly *danseuse* who had once worked with the likes of Balanchine and Graham. A solitary, she'd withdrawn into a small cabin on the lake about a mile from Lawrence's. Katiana told Laura about her Paris years, her affair with Gato Barbieri, the jazzman, whom she'd often found to be "a handful of *merde*" and "the folly of my life." Laura quoted her, mimicking her French accent. Katiana had also known James Baldwin, Marguerite Duras, and Anais Nin in Paris.

"She showed me a picture of herself holding hands with Duras in the Luxembourg Garden." Katiana had invited Laura to travel to Paris "to meet everyone," although in reality everyone had passed on. "It's ironic. Katiana wants to commune with ghosts, but I didn't tell her I'm one."

"Maybe I could go with you next time you visit the old gal," I suggested. "I'd love to meet her."

"No," Laura replied, "she wouldn't like that." Without further explanation she continued to describe Katiana. "Sometimes I imagine Katiana back in Paris, haunting the narrow streets and the cobble stones on the *rive gauche*, living in the Paris of yesterday. I may go with her. She and I could be ghosts together."

On another evening she told me about Bill.

"Allen, you and this cabin remind me of when I'd sit with Bill," she said one rainy evening, referring to Bill Evans, the jazz pianist who died in 1980. But it was 1946 in Laura's story. "I remember sitting with Bill on the screened-in porch of a camp on a bayou near Hammond. Cabins are called camps in Louisiana. We watched the rain hurry toward us along the water to whisper in the cypress and the oaks and then come to us as mist through the torn screen, the mist and the screen veiling the outside world. Then Bill said that whenever it rains you can remember every time it's ever rained. I suppose memory comes alive in those moments when the world wears a veil. Do you remember that poem by Paul Verlaine?

Il pleure dans mon coeur	[Tears in my heart
Comme il pluet sur la ville;	Like rain through the town;
Quelle est cette langeure	What is this pain
Qui penetre mon coeur?	That drowns my years?]

"Bill was right. I still remember the rainy afternoon in the square in Avignon, where I told Petrarch to leave me alone or I'd hire thugs. I almost felt sorry for him as he walked away in the rain. I never saw him again. What stirs inside you in the rain," she said, "isn't something alien. It's what you've always been but may have forgotten. Rain settles into the grooves of your mind and pulls music out, like a needle in an old phonograph. Rain is my dream sound.

"I was 18 when I came back from being dead. Ghosts don't age, and I've been 18 for a very long time. Bill was 17 in 1946. He'd come to Hammond from New Jersey to study music. He played Johnny Mercer's 'Laura' for me one night. I didn't tell him I'd known Johnny, but I think Bill understood I was a ghost. When he left Hammond, I went to the bottom of the bayou and waited many months in the dark water before returning. I couldn't die. Above, the stars were nails poking into the coffin where I lived. I loved Bill."

Another time she told me of haunting the recording sessions Evans did with Miles Davis, the sessions that produced *Kind of Blue*.

"They recorded in an abandoned church in New York that had become the 30th Street Studio for Columbia Records. I hovered in a corner, a shadow within a shadow. As he played, I could see Bill's thoughts swirl about him like smoke. A few years later, I was in Webster Hall when Bill recorded *Alone*. His left arm was half paralyzed from hitting a nerve with a needle, and he had lost weight. I cried my little ghost tears, and as he shuffled to the piano I whispered to him about the bayou and the rain. He played 'Here's that Rainy Day,' the notes weaving themselves into the silence like mist on water."

Once I asked Laura about the scar on her face. What was it a ghost of? Her look darkened, and I didn't ask again. But a couple of evenings before she left me we lay sprawled in front of the fire in the cabin, and she told me that after Bill's death she had decided to haunt the world in the rain. She had drifted down rain-drenched trails in the Green Mountains of Vermont as boas of mist wrapped themselves around trees. She had stretched herself thin on the deck of a boat under a summer shower in Brittany.

"I love Europe," she said. "Everything is old there, haunted...weighted with remembrances and with life gone by...with things the past has left behind. What is most real are the ruins, the ancient stone walls leaning together...the grand sweep of the Coliseum, the broken Arch of Septimius Severus, the Alban Mountains in the distance.

"So few things are haunted in America. There's a strange beauty to rain in forgotten places," she mused, "in bays where ships no longer go. Sometimes in America, you sense that beauty in abandoned drive-in theaters with just a section of the screen still standing, the screen that had reflected so many of yesterday's dreams, and a few old poles leaning out of long grass. Our Europe is old drive-in theaters.

"One rainy day in Portland, I sat by an old woman in a restaurant, watching her thoughts dissolve in the air. She was alone, and time had abandoned her. I wondered if, had I lived, I would have attained a lovely loneliness like hers. Then I drifted away, passing a young couple on the street huddled under an umbrella, in love for a while."

"You are searching," I said, "but you don't want to be seen."

"And you know this about me how?"

"The way you sat in back in the classroom...on the shaded side. The way you hovered in a shadow during the recording session of *Kind of Blue*. The way you refuse to wear makeup. And how you love lonely places...and the veil of rain. You let the world haunt you."

"If I'm secretive, why did I tell you I'm a ghost?"

"I don't know why."

"Are you certain that I did? Perhaps I sensed that you wanted me to be a ghost. You wanted something to write about, so I invented it...Petrarch, Evans, the whole little tale."

"But why would I want you to be a ghost?"

"There are strange yearnings."

"No," I said, "things stay with us, and the past is never dead. Ghosts are here to remind us of that. You're a ghost."

Three

"*Quackity,* quack, quack!" Laura pawed through shelves and drawers.

"You a duck today?" I asked, glancing up from my laptop.

"I'm looking for the duck tape. Moby has a bo-bo." A paperback fluttered down from a shelf like a shot bird. "I found it!"

Laura pivoted and marched off with the tape, a Florence Nightingale about to give first aid—and last aid, as it turned out—to Moby Duck, the rubber ducky who had travelled with her since...whenever. As she disappeared into the bedroom, I admired yet again the tattoo of Zombie, her cat, creeping up to peer mischievously over the back of her jeans, the real Zombie padding along behind her.

Then, two days later, I returned from a walk to find a note duct-taped to the refrigerator door:

> *Allen, I came back to earth for the rain and the music. It isn't your fault that I don't find them now. We ghosts dull easily, and it's time for me to 'Turn Out the Stars' (that's a Bill Evans tune, by the way). Take care of Moby Duck—he has a bo-bo on his tummy. Don't worry about Zombie. He's with me. Oh, and good luck with that novel!*

Perhaps she had been serious about going to Paris with Katiana, and maybe they were still preparing for their trip. Katiana's reason for not wanting to meet me did not matter now. I started down the shoreline, following an off-again-on-again path through trees and brambles. The cabin was empty.

It was empty and had been unoccupied for months if not years, its door hanging askew from a rusted hinge, the screens torn, and the porch rotting and unsafe. The inside was a mausoleum of dust, cobwebs, and the shells of dead insects, but I was sure that the footprints in the dust were Laura's. Something about the room, perhaps the position of the ancient fireplace and of a battered sofa, fit her descriptions, but her imagination had furnished the room with photos and drawings—the picture of Katiana and Duras, a lithograph by Picasso, phonograph records of Gato Barbieri. And of course she had invented a character named Katiana.

I stood for a long while in that dark and empty space trying to visualize the room and the character as Laura had created them. Whatever longing had brought her back from death in the 14th century had not been satisfied by what reality had to offer. Dreams and imaginings were necessary for her, as they are for the living, and her imagination had imposed a world and a history upon the dingy, nondescript little cabin. If Laura was part muse and part ghost, it was no wonder she left me. I couldn't be her instrument. I wasn't up to it. I realized in a flash that my novel was stillborn.

I have an ordinary heart, which broke in the ordinary way—too many cigarettes, too much beer, and a few nights in bars where old men whispered to one another through gray teeth that leaned together like Laura's European walls. Her strange stories had touched me with their soft wings of yearning. And then she was gone. Over the following months I gave up writing. I gave up imagination.

My brother and his bride are back from their honeymoon in Europe, back at work in Minneapolis. And I have an office next door to a business school and overlooking the Lakewalk in Duluth, where people, in summer, bike in spandex and jog in cotton. At lunch hour, there is usually a man riding a unicycle.

We make educational products for children—games, computers, etc. I'm in PR, writing letters and giving talks. The word nerd. I'm over my romance with the sacred realms of art and imagination. I sell things made of plastic. And when books or movies talk about the heightened realities peopled by poets and musicians, those people are like ghosts in the rain to me. They don't live in my world. I may try to write again, although I suspect that this is my last story. To me, now, salvation lies in ordinary and dependable things. They are the stepping stones on life's rapids.

When I swivel my chair toward the window and look out over the Lakewalk toward the Aerial-Lift Bridge, when I watch the clouds limp along the Wisconsin shore like ghosts gone lame, and when I prop my feet up by Moby Duck (The symbol of my years of writing is a rubber duck!) and listen to Bill Evans play "My Foolish Heart" on my iPod, my longings are vague and unimportant. I suppose we need our small mental vacations, our ghosts and dreams, but only because they lead us quickly back to work.

There are kids out there who benefit by our products. One is a video game I helped create in which Moby Duck is now a character. It's good work, and there's redemption in good work, a truth that was bred into the family genes and that has finally surfaced in me as well. Even on his post card showing a narrow stone walkway in Gordes in the Luberon, Lawrence mentioned getting back to America and work. We weren't born to dream the time away.

Will I see Laura again? Maybe when I'm old and work is finished, I'll visit Avignon to walk near the Papal Palace and Sainte-Claire—perhaps, and if I'm fortunate, there'll be rain. I'll search the faces. Maybe I'll write then about lost places and times, about abandoned things. Perhaps she'll be my muse after all, when I've become one of those abandoned things.

For now, though, I'll keep my thoughts at home. Once in a while I'll meet Laura in some dingy old cabin of the mind or heart, but I know that in the meantime her footsteps will echo down other halls and her laughter will float on other summer nights. Other people will have their Lauras, and some also will write about her. It's all one song. I wish them well.

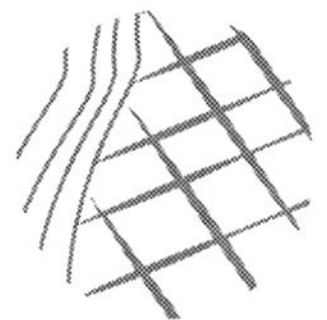

The House on Hawthorne Road

They sit on the grass by a pond in a small park near the College of St. Scholastica. In the distance, down a tree-lined path, a statue of Jesus with arms held high guards the front of the administration building. In the other direction, the monastery rests between green and yellow hills beneath clouds like crushed pearls. Jean wears a peasant skirt and sits with her knees tucked beneath it. A copy of *The Reindeer Camps* rests in the grass beside her. The man is dressed in blue jeans and a polo shirt, and a few feet away a boy in a blue Twins cap side-arms pieces of bread into the pond.

Birdsong sparkles in the trees. Jean's eyes follow the ducks as they paddle here and there, bobbing for the bread that floats among remnants of last autumn's leaves. On the far side of the pond, near a gazebo, a great blue heron stands rooted in a splash of marsh marigold and a willow tree lets its branches down to the water. Two crows alight on a branch of a poplar above the heron. The time is spring.

"So that's it?" she says or asks.

"Yes. I've got an offer from Cornell. It's huge. I'm out of here in two weeks."

"And what about me? What will I do?"

As the man turns toward her, a chocolate lab ambles by on his way to another tree. Its leash trails like a snake among last year's acorns.

"I suppose your dad will find you a doctor," the man says. "You'll graduate. You'll get old."

Jean watches his face redden as he speaks. *It's the color of ham,* she thinks. She lifts her arm and considers her watch, and then she says that this will be the moment when she learned to hate. This will be the memory that will stay. She says her hatred will be fire.

The boy in the baseball cap flips the last of his bread into the water and turns toward home. In the distance, horns argue on Kenwood Avenue. *They bleat like sheep,* she thinks. Closer by, the new leaves on branches whisper among themselves. A bronze butterfly dozes among them in blue shade. It's wings tremble, and then a breeze lifts it lightly away.

Two

For two hours, after the truck from *RJ Sports* unloaded the yellow moped at the house on Hawthorne Road, Arnie felt both joy and relief—joy over the shinning new scooter and relief that his father had apparently softened. It was a perfect summer day, with a cool breeze off of Lake Superior and a few sheepish clouds lazing about. He took pictures with his Samsun of the new machine parked in the driveway, first with the cherry tree in the background and next before the wrought iron fence. Maybe things were improving. There might even be hugs. A butterfly alighted on a tulip and folded its wings like hands in the ancient attitude of prayer.

Then his father, a prominent urologist, returned home from his office near *St. Luke's Hospital*, the black Lexus swinging aggressively into the driveway like a hearse running late. It stopped beside the moped. As the butterfly took to the air, Dad heaved himself from the car, hitching his pants up as his gaze homed in on Arnie from under eyebrows like dark branches.

He told Arnie it was time for him to leave, to find an apartment. The moped was the last thing Dad intended to do for him, and he even seemed to smile as tears formed in Arnie's eyes. "You're an adult," his father said, making it sound like an accusation. "Lose the craziness and stop sniffling. You need to be someone!"

A year ago, he had made Jean leave the house to have the baby. "If I ever see that baby, I want to see it with a father in tow!" Dad had shouted. She hadn't come back, and the days were long over of Arnie and his little sister, Jean, watching *All in the Family* and *The Cosby Show* on the Persian rug as mother brought mountainous bowls of popcorn, or of them building snowmen as the first snowfall brushed their faces and filled the yard.

In a few days Arnie, perched on his new scooter, prowled the streets of Duluth, dodging pot holes and searching for a place to live, consoling himself all the while that Dad was mean to everyone.

Now, on a Saturday in June three years after his own exile from the home on Hawthorne, Arnie repeats his Saturday morning ritual, donning his red beret, locking the door of the rented house on Park Point, straddling the yellow moped, hearing the friendly purr of the engine, and then heading for Canal Park. Although alone, he is not always unhappy. He loves Duluth, and especially the bustle of Canal Park.

He leaves the scooter in front of the Dewitt-Seitz Marketplace, an old factory building now renovated to house restaurants and shops. Arnie's first stop is *Hepzibah's*. There he lingers over his selection from the exquisite array of fresh chocolates and confections displayed behind glass—Truffles and Marzipans, Pecan Turtles and Caramel Toasties, Chocolate Maraschinos complete with stems, Pepperitas Habanero looking like pepper by virtue of red and green frosting, and the incomparable Pavarotti, named for the singer—all of them handmade in Duluth.

On other days, he goes to *The Rocky Mountain*

Chocolate Factory across the street, where spectators gather to watch a lovely girl wield a huge spatula to stir the chocolate on a long table as she banters with her audience. It's free and delicious theatre, a part of Duluth's effort to re-invent itself as a vacation destination.

Today in *Hepzibah's*, a very large man with a blue notebook jots down the names of the various confections. He steps aside, smiling, "I need to know the names for a story I'm writing," he says. Arnie completes his selection at the counter and adds a coffee-to-go. "Thank you, love," the lady behind the counter says as always. The first time she had called him "love," his face had blossomed with a blush, but the goose-bump moment withered when she added, "Don't worry, I'm Irish. I call everyone love."

Arnie steps outside to sit on the sundeck and watch the tourists and the residents go about the drama called Saturday. Some enter *Grandma's Saloon and Grill* for their morning coffee, some head for the *Maritime Visitor Center* by the canal, their cameras and children dangling from their arms, and still others turn the corner toward the *Duluth Pack Store* with its jackets, camping gear, and the grand, shellacked canoe hanging from the ceiling. By the flea market across the street, a small crowd gathers to watch a man play a bagpipe while riding a unicycle. It is all part of the drama, and Arnie plays the part of audience.

Last Saturday Arnie made his yearly tour of the *S.S. William A. Irvin*, docked nearby and open to the public. Now retired, it had once been the flag ship of

U.S. Steel's Great Lakes Fleet. Today, Arnie watches a distant ship glide toward the canal, pushing a white-cap before it—perhaps a ship like the *Edmund Fitzgerald*, the "laker" that went down in a storm years ago, killing so many sailors.

Often Arnie dreams of the ghosts of the sailors sunk deep in the water but then emerging into culverts and up into the city's sewer system, their fingers protruding from grates in the streets like the fingers of Orson Wells in *The Third Man*. As today's ship, a freighter from Russia, arrives safely, the Aerial-Lift Bridge rises to allow the ship passage into the harbor where grain and ore can be loaded, more grain than ore these days, since the Iron Range has fallen on hard times. As always, sea gulls, squawking like kazoos, circle about the watchtower at the far end of the canal.

Tourists pass on the sidewalk in front of the sundeck where Arnie sits. A small girl clings to her father's hand. "Daa-ad, you said we could go to the zoo and ..." The complaint dies in the blast of a car horn. Then a nearby cell phone plays its tune, pulling Arnie's attention away from the approaching freighter and the birds. He listens to half of a conversation: "Amanda Persons, the writer?...Somers Lounge...Friday? Sure...Okay, pick me up ..." *So many lives,* Arnie thinks, *doing so many things.*

A woman in leather rounds the corner on a Honda Gold Wing, her hair free in the wind. Arnie looks away, embarrassed as she parks her big bike near his moped. His eyes move to the corner of the sundeck, where Deborah had set up her easel every weekend during the previous summer. Her charcoal drawings had been popular, and she was equally adept at realism, caricature, or flattery. Over a period of months, Arnie had bought a number of drawings from her, and an entire section of his wall at home had become a small gallery of charcoal Arnies.

He had enjoyed conversations with Deborah, her head always tipped to the left and her hair falling across her right eye. He remembers her moves, and today he remembers how she had explained that the artist mustn't fear mistakes.

"A mistake can always be turned into art," she'd said. A smudge on the paper can become a tree in the background, and a faulty line on a face can create an inspired expression. "Knowing that one can always make good use of a mistake is liberating." Arnie had found her words strange.

Then one day she said goodbye. She and her friend were moving to Boston, where the friend would study architecture. Arnie's sister, Jean, had moved from the large house on Hawthorne. She had her baby, Arnie's niece Rebecca, and eventually made a civil union with Roberta Rollins, the founder of a well-known women's clinic in a suburb of Minneapolis. And Arnie had moved to Park Point. But for Deborah to move to a different state! To Boston! The news had been both sad and terrifying.

"There is a poem by Theodore Roethke," Deborah had said, "where he writes: *I learn by going where I have to go.* I love that. Going is nothing to be afraid of, Arnie. Besides, we'll make a living in Boston."

Arnie removes his glasses. As the world blurs, his

thoughts become more clear. He thinks about Deborah. Her odd ideas. Her recklessness. He knows that things change, that stock prices fluctuate and brunettes become blondes. Dad had owned a Studebaker once, a car that no longer exists. Mom had worn penny-loafers in her youth. Years later, Jean had gotten breast implants! But to Arnie, the good life is in familiar things, in always finding *Hepzibah's* open on Saturday, always buying a book at *Northern Lights*. The good life is like Coca-Cola, always the same.

He puts on his glasses, feeling the weight of the thick lenses on his nose and the pressure of the bow behind his right ear. Things focus. He scratches his arm, a habit that had always annoyed his father.

"We've been to Dr. Anderson," Dad had said. "He tested for a zillion allergies and found nothing. So stop all that damned scratching. There's nothing there!"

Arnie lets the memory drift away like clouds over the lake. He thinks about Canal Park, which he loves and hopes will never change. Then, after enjoying his Pavarotti and coffee, he re-enters the DeWitt-Seitz to visit his favorite shops, beginning on the third floor with *Christian Eggert Violins*, the name written in black script by the door, and then proceeding down the hall to *Rosewood Music*, specializing in guitars and guitar repair. Arnie has always dreamed of playing either a cello or a classical guitar, but somehow has never taken the first step.

Downstairs, he visits *Art Doc*, with its various pieces by local artists: potters and jewelers, weavers and photographers, makers of leaded glass and carvers of wood. He especially admires the photographs of Lake Superior, its summer shoreline and the amazing winter-ice formations. Water, so frightening in reality, can nonetheless be lovely in a photograph. *Art Doc* is another new store for tourists, and sometimes Arnie likes to think that he, too, is a tourist.

Near *Art Doc*, a woman and a small child descend the stair toward a restaurant called *Amazing Grace*.

"Mommy, can I have milk and animal quackers?"

Arnie passes the stair and emerges outside as a quick morning shower ends and the last raindrops are children on holiday skipping down the street. *Oh what a beautiful morning!* The words of the song tumble in his mind. He straightens his beret and strolls through the flea market that occupies a portion of the parking lot.

He loves to muse over the costumes and props of past lives, to finger faded shirts, cracked cups and saucers, and vinyl records in disintegrating jackets. He imagines a deathbed scene where a loved one places a favorite album beneath an old needle for the last time. Sometimes Arnie buys an album, perhaps something by Frank Sinatra, shown with a jaunty hat and one arm raised in the body language of song, or maybe Joan Baez, barefoot on the beach at Big Sur. For half an hour each Saturday, Arnie is an archeologist of life's dreams, brooding over tables of tools and artifacts, sensing the mysteries of other people's stories, hearing their soft, sad melodies.

In the past, Arnie would select a book each Saturday at *Northern Lights Books and Gifts*, his reading for the week, but now the store has departed, just as Deborah has with her easel, and the space once filled with books is just a clutter of toys for toddlers with sticky hands.

Arnie buys a bag of peaches from a one-legged man by a green cart with a sign saying "Veteran" stuck to its side. Then he crosses the street to sit by the canal, opening his mind to his surroundings as his hand gropes in the bag. A smear of bubble gum adorns the sidewalk, and further off a pigeon eats pizza. Two girls walk by, stirring the air with laughter. One drops a crumpled candy wrapper by Arnie's feet. He scratches his arm, watching the wrapper open slowly, blossoming. The ship has passed through the canal, and the lift bridge completes its descent.

Minutes pass, and then Arnie notices the large man from *Hepzibah's* on a nearby bench, tapping his pen on an open page of his blue notebook. The gesture brings back an ancient fear implanted by his father, who, on a sunny morning at the breakfast table, had once said that Arnie was like a goofy character in a TV cartoon. It revisits Arnie like sudden rain, the fear that he is not real but merely a minor character in someone else's story or play. Or cartoon. The man on the bench looks up and nods to Arnie, his many chins tumbling down his neck. *Can I stand and walk away now,* Arnie wonders, *or would he have to write it in his notebook first?*

The man returns to his writing, and Arnie walks back to the DeWitt-Seitz Marketplace, steps into his moped, and turns in behind a line of cars obediently nudging toward Superior Street. It's time to ride to *Saint Mary's Hospital...*no, now it's called *Essentia...* where Mom, who once starred with the *Duluth Rep,* plays her final scene. He finds her bivouacked among the usual accessories of disease, and today he also sees that tubes have been added, tubes coming from her nose like noodles.

"They're for oxygen," Nurse Wilfred explains before continuing her rounds of mercy.

The dozen roses that Arnie sent yesterday keep silent vigil on the nightstand. As he inhales their fragrance, Mom's hand struggles heroically with bedding and tubing, emerging at last to where he can fondle her ancient knuckles as duty and affection dictate. He snatches his red beret from his head and perches on the edge of the bed, feet dangling above the floor like pendants. He takes her hand and fumbles for a topic. A pungent silence.

"Mom," he finally asks, "remember when Grandma died? They used oxygen tents then, and the first time you took me to see her I thought she was trapped in a bubble of goo. Remember?" Her face scrunches, perhaps into a smile. He continues: "And the way she was propped at that odd angle and doing those squiggly things with her eyebrows, she looked like that William F. Buckley guy you and Dad always admired! We could have put her in a talent show right there in the hospital, and she would have won hands down. Buckley-in-a-Bag! Then, when she'd pout, she looked like a little fish in a plastic baggy ready to come home from the store. But I don't know what you look like with all your tubes. Maybe like an oyster in spaghetti. I wish I had my camera! "

She gurgles appreciatively until a bubble grows from around the noodle in one nostril. Arnie weighs her hand in his, not knowing what to say and watching Mom's nose through many eruptive cycles. It is time for words of love and consolation, time to return ancient favors, nose-wiping favors and everything-will-be-all-right favors. As he cleans his glasses, his unaided eyes soften her to a blur.

"It's okay, Mom. You've had a good life, and now you're gurgling and melting. But the docs here at *St. Mary's...Essentia*...will do their best. I'm going to ask Doc Melville to slip something in your I.V. to grease the slide. No fun just lingering in the noodles, right? Might as well move on to the next performance. I called *Williams-Lobermeier Funeral Home* and told them it's two outs and two strikes in the bottom of the ninth. And guess what! They're ready anytime! How's that for service? And I got Lars—remember Lars, who published that poem in the paper when the sled dogs died? I got Lars to write a eulogy. So don't worry. I'll say Lars's eulogy, then whoosh! Mom Among the Noodles will be Ashes in a Jug. It's amazing!"

It's the sort of joking that he and his mother had enjoyed in the old days, inventing outlandish scenarios, but now it feels inappropriate, more a compulsion than a joke. *What am I doing? I'm thirty-nine years old!* He feels like an actor who has blundered into the wrong scene. *Why must I always be the clown?* But it's too late to stop. He must play out the scene. Salvage it. He shifts his weight, still clutching her hand, and puts his glasses back on. She comes into focus in a pocket of silence.

"And then you've got eternity. Just think of it, rocking eternity! Do you know how long that is? Have you heard the one about the bird carrying one grain of sand at a time to the moon? No, make that the far side of Andromeda! By the time he gets all the sand in the world up there, eternity is still a show waiting to happen. Lady Gaga is still in the dressing room! Do you know how much sand there is? Think beaches and bunkers. Think hacky-sacks. Think Nevada and New Mexico. And all that time is yours! With nothing to do! You'll just sit there under an umbrella like the head official in tennis and look down on all the future. You'll know what incredible things people think centuries form now. How they like their eggs. If it's still the Vikings vs. the Packers. If Brett Favre stays retired. You'll know the mysteries of space and time, like if they shovel their walks on Neptune or eat lefsa on Venus."

Silence.

This isn't working, he tells himself. *Whose script is this?*

"You know what Oscar Wilde said on his death bed? He was staring at the crappy wallpaper, and he said, 'One of us has to go'. How cool is that?! Now stop blowing bubbles, Mom. I know you're excited about moving on, and as I said, I'll talk to Doc Melville. I'll slip him a twenty for alacrity, for wings for my angel. Because you have been an angel, Mom, and next time you go to sleep you might wake up flapping feathers with that little bird. You might even get to carry a grain of sand!" Then, placing her hand in the bedding and stroking her head, he adds, "Still, you better fix your makeup. There might be reincarnation."

With her tubes and her hair in tangles, with the

bedding rumpled, her small face, pale and pocked, is like a Maxfli in the rough. He remembers the peaches.

"By the way, Mom," he says, bringing her back from a distant shore, "I brought you some peaches, but it looks like they drip everything in you now, so I'll just leave one here by the roses as a symbol. Unless you want me to mush it into your I.V. bag? No? Well, I'm off then. What's that? Your swan song is kind of slurred. You're just snorting away at the gates of hog heaven. But if you could talk at all, I bet you could tell some stories now—or soon!" He slides off the bed and places his ear close to her face. "Oh, that's all right, Mom. Think nothing of it. Kiss-kiss, you old slugabed you."

I'm truly insane, he thinks as he walks down the corridor to the elevator, recognizing the old smells of medicines and chemicals. Hanging like a gargoyle on the side of the bed, Arnie had babbled about cremation and eternity. *I'm a lunatic in a bad movie,* he thinks, but hadn't Mom always called him her little clown? *Mom understands.* In the elevator, a woman holds the hand of a small boy.

"Remember, Jimmy, Dr. Moen will make you all well, and when you get big you can be anything you want."

"Do I have to?"

As Arnie rides his moped back toward Park Point, the potholes jostle up memories of the home on Hawthorne Road, the mansion with its wrought-iron fence draped with clematis, its brick wall, the gardens that bled flowers each spring, the maples and cedars. During the summers there had been hide-and-seek in the yard, and in winters snowmen and forts and gently falling flakes, always with so many friends, neighborhood kids, the children of doctors and lawyers and even the mayor. One woman had nine children, and Arnie's mother used to whisper "biblically fertile" when the woman herded her brood down the sidewalk, and when the yard filled with neighborhood kids Mom called them "the begotten."

In the evening in the spring, his mother would say that the stars were like crocuses blooming in the garden of the sky, and then, with Arnie nestled by her side, she'd create story time and joke time. She had taught Arnie and Jean to "read" the Tarot, although it was really just a matter of inventing stories using characters from the deck. The days rolled by like brightly painted figures on a merry-go-round. But now his childhood friends have all run off to hide in their adult lives, their careers and families, and Arnie is still "It."

He remembers the time one of Mom's college friends came to visit. She had looked down, extended a hand, smiled, and said, "You must be Arnie!" It was a clarifying moment. Yes, he had no choice. He had to be Arnie.

And then, only a few days later, he fell from a boat while he and Dad fished at Island Lake. Instead of reaching for him immediately, Dad laughed as he groped for his camera to take a picture of Arnie thrashing in the waves. A decade down the road, Dad still grinned while telling the story of "adorkable Arnie's *YouTube* moment." Mother's friend, smiling down and extending her hand, and Dad, towering above the water laughing, still alternate in Arnie's dreams, one face dissolving into the other.

One day, in a better mood on the fourth fairway at *Northland Country Club*, Dad had offered advice on choosing a wife: "A woman's beauty means reproductive health. Check her teeth, son. Check the curve of her thighs. And hooters matter! You want a babe who'll throw good pups. The future demands it. Our genes are the gift we owe tomorrow! So get laid, my boy—get laid, or I'll have your little wiener examined! Now step back and let Doc Whiz show you how to knock down a six iron into the wind."

On other days, when Arnie retreated to his room and his video games, his dad joked about his periodic "nerdgasms." That was the summer when Dad sported a narrow beard that looped under his chin like bread crust. Arnie had imagined taking a bite.

Years later, when Arnie had already passed the age at which other young men—the begotten—were earning incomes and starting families, Dad insisted that he rent his own house, using the trust fund his mother had created for him. Dad would become angry and shout, "Normal up, Arnie! Normal up! You can't be a nerd all your life. You're over thirty now! Decide who you are! Be somebody! And stop that damned scratching!" He almost hoisted Arnie onto the new moped and pushed him down the winding, hillside road. The scene plays over and over on memory's stage.

Over time, his dad made him feel that everything he did was a crazy mistake. What had made Deborah, carelessly heading off to Boston, so blasé about mistakes? Even now, Arnie often wonders if he's holding his fork or tying his shoe properly. Dad became the Chief Critic of his life, and his only lesson had been that Arnie would never know the right thing to do.

On the rainy night before Dad's death in the front bedroom, the oak tree rapped its old knuckles against the house like some gnarled and ghastly messenger. The light in Dad's eyes had gone dull and vague, sunk in murky waters. Sunk like those sailors on the lake. But then the light swam back to the surface long enough for him to rise on one elbow, lift his other arm theatrically, and intone about genes and marriage and Arnie's penis. A line of sweat had clung to Dad's cheek like something left by a snail. Arnie stood by the bed scratching his arm in defiance.

His younger sister, Jean, still visits Arnie occasionally, bringing her laughter and her freckles back to his life. But she has her child, Rebecca, and lives with her companion on the grounds of the clinic near Minneapolis. Arnie would be the last Ellsworth on Hawthorne Road. The years had wandered by, dressing and undressing themselves, and still, in dreams, Dad lectures down at him, his huge eyebrows in constant motion like branches over pools. And still on lonely afternoons, Arnie wonders who is writing his life into a notebook no one will read, a play no one will see.

He knows he will miss his mother, miss the days filled with the joy she took in her acting, in her garden, in the summer vacations to Pacific islands and European cities. After Dad died, she took in a friend at the house, and the house keeper stayed on. But she had not asked

Arnie to come home until now, now that the house was empty. Last week, before her speech became swamped in mucus for her final curtain call, Mom made him promise to move back to the family home. "I want you to keep the lights on," she said in a way that did not refer to electricity.

It stays light until 9:00 p.m. in June by Lake Superior, but the weather is changeable. A summer morning can become a near-winter afternoon. Now, as he rides, Arnie feels the old chill return to the air, and as he crosses the lift bridge he dares not look down at the water waiting below. Dark clouds tug themselves across the lake like chain mail. Wind pushes his scooter about, adding to the slipperiness of the grating on the bridge. His red beret leaps from his head and swirls off into the harbor, where the Russian ship is now anchored. Cranes have been positioned for unloading.

Finally, standing on his porch fumbling for the key, Arnie listens to the intensity of the waves rearing and tumbling on the lakeside shore. He enters, locking the door behind him.

He holds each of his three peaches to his nose, and then arranges them in a row on the piano. Soon there will be another urn standing guard on the mantel in the library of the old home beneath the portrait of Grandfather Ellsworth, whose old-money gaze always chilled the air. Perhaps the ashes in the urns will whisper to one another. Grandfather Ellsworth was one of the last men to make a fortune in lumbering, one of the people who finished the project of destroying all the old-growth pines in northern Minnesota. Would

Arnie dare to take down Grandfather's portrait?

Now he plays a familiar scene yet again. Standing in the middle of his room in Park Point, Arnie is surrounded by pictures, the gallery of his life. The walls are crowded with Arnies, each photo framed and blurred by dust. The exhibit is arranged as a narrative. To the right of the front door, a bustling nursery covers the wall. A spanking new Arnie is seen through the glass of a hospital viewing room, and then a baby Arnie bides his time in his mother's arms, a pacifier plugged in his mouth.

As the living Arnie moves along the wall, the pictured Arnie grows older: Arnie under the maple tree with his first red wagon; Arnie and Jean at the beach with shovels and buckets, smiles spread across their tanned faces like butter on toast; Arnie and Jean, their faces gazing up into softly falling snow, making angels in the yard; Arnie and a neighbor girl, one of the begotten, wielding golf clubs by the lilacs, "playing doctor," as his mother used to say to tease Dad. Each photo is a piece of time nicked off by the camera and preserved under glass.

Arnie pauses by his old stereo and lowers the needle onto Mussorgsky's famous suite. Then he continues to the back wall, which offers scenes of his first trip to Europe when he was eleven years old—a photo of Arnie and his mother in front of the Tuleries Palace in Paris, one of Arnie and a toddling Jean in the marketplace of Limoges, and another of them at the entrance to the Catacombs in Rome. And a fourth picture with a corner torn off, apparently taken by a helpful stranger, shows both children and both parents in front of an old castle somewhere in Europe.

Moving along the wall, he next sees photos of himself at Marshal Preparatory and then at the College of St. Scholastica, where he played Puck in the yearly Shakespeare production. Then, as he comes up the adjacent wall toward the front of the room, the pictured Arnies approach the age of the viewing Arnie. He gazes at scenes of himself with elderly parents, at two shots of himself by his father's coffin, Dad lying as straight and proper as an Oscar, Arnie scratching. Soon he will stand by his mother's coffin. *Who will take that picture?* he wonders.

After the funeral pictures, in a special place to the left of the front door, Deborah's charcoal drawings converse among themselves or merely doze in their frames. He is delighted at the many poses she found for him, as though there were many Arnies. In one drawing his head is bare and he cradles a camera artistically. In another he wears his red beret at a snappy angle like Frank Sinatra. In a third he carries a bag of peaches, and in a fourth he reads a book from *Northern Lights.*

In each drawing the shops of Canal Park recede in the background. The sameness of the setting is comforting, and the many Arnies offer the hope of various possibilities within the one Arnie who always smiled back at Deborah, and now at himself. It is strange that life can appear so pleasant when rendered in photos and drawings.

As the Mussorgsky record ends, he realizes that his day and his life have spun in circles. His days are circles within a circle, and he has spiraled toward a still center like the grooves of a vinyl record. What would it have been like to marry? To have become a lawyer? A priest? He fumbles with his days like the beads of a rosary. His thoughts of Deborah mingle with thoughts of Mom and then with the memory of a melody. Will he be seeing them in all the old familiar places? Will he return to the house on Hawthorne, home for Christmas? As a child, he had always kept the lights on at night in his room. But now, how will he keep the lights on in the way Mom had meant? It is all a circle, sometimes frightening like a whirlpool pulling you down, other times gentle like a phonograph record turning out an old song. Circles within circles on a circling planet.

This room is my life, he thinks, *my life and my mind.*

He stands motionless for a long time in the center of the room, framed by the doorway and surrounded by pictures of his past and of the selves he left behind or never became. Dead selves in their coffins. The narrative is finished. He removes his glasses, and the pictures dissolve. The air in his room dims further as in a theatre, and outside, gathering itself over the lake, the ghost of winter prepares its entrance. The thought of the empty house on Hawthorne Road brings a wave of panic. There will be ghosts whispering and shuffling. He cannot go back. He inhales the darkness that rises about him like water. *I've drowned*, he thinks. *Finally I've drowned.* The panic subsides. *Finally,* he thinks with relief, *I'm no one.*

Three

Jean had determined never to return to Duluth, but now, driving north on I-35, she exited just beyond Hinckley to finish the trip on Highway 23, the old scenic route she had nearly memorized during trips to and from The Cities in her college days. The car itself seemed to know the familiar curves, and it slowed of its own, as if in respect, as it passed the makeshift cross where a young girl had died. *Rhonda*, Jean remembered, *eleven years old*. And it was the car that decided to stop at the scenic overlook above the vast St. Louis River Valley.

It was November, with rusting leaves everywhere and hints of winter in the air even though no significant snow had yet fallen. She sat in a Carhartt jacket on the concrete railing above the valley, remembering the spring day at St. Scholastica when she glanced at her watch and declared that she would never forget that moment. The moment when she learned to hate. But things change, and now the hatred was only another ash in memory's fireplace.

During the past summer, on the third Thursday of each month, women in her new network came together at the clinic as a support group. For a recent meeting, those convalescing from experiences with men had agreed to share their stories. One girl, an attractive student from the University of St. Thomas, had talked about "the eternal subtext," by which she meant the theme of sex and mating that often lurks beneath the surface of conversations between men and women.

An older man she had met recently had hinted over lunch of his wealth, saying, "Yes, I travel to Europe from time to time." She had craftily made him clarify that the trips were not with a wife. Next she heard that he'd been on his university's swim team. *He's bragging*, she had thought, *which means he's interested.* She rewarded him by leaning forward, allowing her breasts to spill a bit toward him.

"It was like I was offering him two scoops of vanilla." The other women laughed and nodded knowingly. "Anyway," the girl continued, "the words on the surface vary, but the text below the surface is always the same."

The girl's take on flirting had prompted others to share experiences, and the wine they also shared made each girl's story more entertaining. It had been a lively evening of bonding. Now, gazing out from the scenic overlook, Jean realized that she had written herself out of that particular subtext. She was no longer a character in the man-woman drama scripted by our culture. She was free, authoring herself. She checked the time on her phone, climbed back into her Accord, and completed the drive to Duluth.

After crossing the lift bridge from Canal Park to Park Point, she stood for a moment on Arnie's porch with her face turned upward to receive the gentle snow that fluttered down in a windless, late-November afternoon, warming quickly to drops on her neck and cheeks. Soon, Duluth would dish out a harsher version of winter, but the early snows were soft and lovely things, "pieces of the stars" her mother had said once. The cars parked on Arnie's street were ghosted with a thin layer of snow. Jean rang the doorbell, and her brother answered. She was saddened by the first hints of gray in his hair.

As they removed Arnie's photo's from the wall, they paused before the one of their mother sitting on a lawn with her grandfather and grandmother, Jean and Arnie's great-grandparents. Arnie had kept this one in a special place on the mantle. It was dated Veterans Day, 1944, when their mother was three years old.

"Do you remember Mom's story about this picture?" Jean asked.

"Yes," Arnie said. "It was about the end of a war. She had talked about swallows in the air. 'Lacing the air,' she said."

"Yes. She lived in a small town in Iowa with her grandparents then, and her own Mom worked in another town."

Each of them fell silent, remembering their mother's voice:

> *I sat by Grandma on the lawn and heard her talk of Calvary—of the thing called passion on a cross and of how they found the rock rolled away and the tomb empty. While she talked, I'd glance at Granddad sinking in his chair and gazing across the gravel road. His eyes were the gray of distant smoke, and the days seemed to fall about his feet with the leaves from the elms. He'd fought in WWI and came home to be a small-town doctor. He had cared well for people for years. Maybe that's why I married a doctor.*
>
> *And as Grandma talked, Polio Willy might limp by, small and quiet as a moth. He would*

dissolve down the darkening path and vanish at his mother's gate. To me, that autumn was about the going away of things, the migrating hawks and geese, the leaves curling about their own shadows, the dog that ran away. And my dad dead in the war.

Then drops of starlight touched the sky... like drops of milk, I used to think...and insects whispered in the grass. I imagined they whispered about my lost father, the war we'd won, and all the love left unfinished.

Jean and Arnie saw themselves reflected in the glass of the photo.

"Our dad was so mean," Arnie said, "not like Mom's father, who was a hero."

"Meanness as punctual as midnight," Jean agreed. "But Arnie, it's time to forgive him and let go. He couldn't help it. His mind was sick, and he couldn't have feelings for others. It's called sociopathy, and not even psychiatrists can help. If you forgive him, you'll feel better. You'll be free. If you don't, he'll continue to torment you. You don't need to scratch that itch anymore."

Arnie mentioned his mother, always laboring gallantly to keep her sadness out of sight, hidden beneath the imagined worlds of her acting in the *Duluth Rep*.

"Her acting was like the synthetic gloves doctors and nurses wear," Jean said, "protection against the pus and blood."

On the wall beside the mantle was the picture of

Jean and Arnie at the entrance to the Catacombs in Rome when they were children. Arnie was eleven and had been frightened by the legend of the old bogie man in the dark recesses of the labyrinth, but Dad had dragged him in anyway, telling him to grow up. But Arnie said nothing today.

"Are you letting it go?" Jean asked. "The word happiness would not mean anything if you don't also know what sadness is. It's time to be happy now."

"Yes."

"You'll have a life now with us at the clinic," Jean said. "You'll have a lovely cabin right on the campus near the pond, and there are hiking trails through the wooded area. We'll decide what things you can do to help out. Maybe you'd like to take care of the grounds, the flowers and the pond and all. You'll have a job. We can't escape from ourselves, but we can find things to do, distracting and pleasant things.

"We'll eat together in the cafeteria, and you'll make friends. You'll be a person. Roberta already loves you, you know, and Rebecca loves her Uncle Arnie. You'll have your moped, and during time off, we can go to movies or museums in The Cities. It'll be a real life, Arnie, and I'm so sorry I haven't been closer to you these last three years. It's been hard starting out... starting a new me. But I've learned tomorrow can be better...You have to believe that."

Arnie remembered the poem Deborah had quoted, the one about learning by going. And he remembered her optimism about her own going to Boston. "I never knew what Dad wanted," he said.

"I didn't either, but you're right. Something was missing for him...or in him."

They held each other for a long moment, standing near the cardboard boxes from Super Value, now containing the many pictures and the charcoal drawings by the street artist, Deborah. They would sort through them back at the clinic in the Metro, and the moped and the piano would be delivered by truck. The rest of Arnie's furnishings had been donated and were already gone.

They'd pass the night in the Sheraton, and unless snow became a problem they would drive back to the Twin Cities the next day. Later, assuming a buyer is found, Jean would return to Duluth to finalize the sale of the house on Hawthorne Road. Jean and Arnie knew they wouldn't spend much time in Duluth from now on. *Maybe*, Arnie thought, *the writer of my life will make it a happier ending. Maybe I'll even have a puppy.*

Their hug ended, and then they carried the boxes out to the car. Their breath made ghosts that mingled with the gently falling snow that touched their faces.

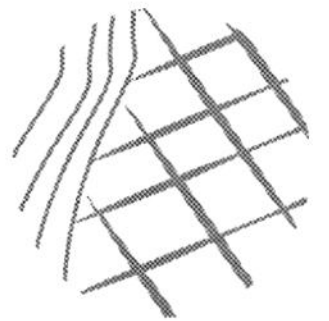

You Must Believe in Spring

When I moved to Duluth, Hal and Amanda, my first friends, were a rich source of tales about life in my newly adopted city, tales that did not always take truth as their primary obligation. They told me about Billy on the evening that Amanda gave a reading from her new book of stories, so maybe Billy was just a fiction too. And then of course there are gaps in my memory that I'll fill in with scraps of my own invention. In short, dear reader, *caveat emptor.*

I'll begin by imagining my two friends in their breakfast nook overlooking a hillside of trees and homes that jostle their way down to Lake Superior. Clouds are stacked in bales over the Wisconsin shore. Amanda's breakfast for the brain, the Sudoku puzzle from the morning paper, is in place beside her bowl of Cheerios. An inveterate worrier, perhaps she mentions our planet's continuing environmental issues. Another hot summer looms. Hal, an inveterate male, may nod absently as he reaches for his orange juice, his disobedient mind conjuring an image of the angular redhead with the tattooed ankle and stiletto heels who ornaments the Cosmetics counter at *Target*. Hal works in Pharmacy, located adjacent to Cosmetics as if to offer alternate services to the flesh.

The topic at the breakfast table turns to the collection of narrated drawings in a brown envelope resting near the juice pitcher, Billy Carlson's fledgling graphic novel tentatively titled *Morph Man*. Knowing that Amanda writes stories and even more miraculously has many of them published, Billy approached Hal and asked if he would have Amanda "see if it sucks." Billy was a homely kid with a small oval body careening about on legs like bent twigs.

"The guy can draw," Hal says to Amanda. The protagonist of *Morph Man* is Clark, who, on the first page, falls in love with a girl viewed from across a pond in a park. Seeing the girl incites Clark's pursuit of transformation. With the aid of potions supplied by a nerdy chemistry student, Clark toils each morning before his bathroom mirror to tug his face and body into more attractive, or at least more interesting, configurations.

From behind the toothpaste splatters on the glass, Clark sees his arms stretch to enormous proportions, even into wings. One morning he manages to pull a horn from his forehead, and on another his ears stretch to the size of satellite dishes. He even learns to assume the shape of various animals. Each night during sleep, his body returns to its old, sad normality, raw material for the next morning's labors.

But Clark's sculpting efforts fail to make him a superhero. His body still limps, still erupts in pimples and boils, and still emits gas with an alarming frequency. He does not dare show himself in public, moping about his dusty apartment instead, perhaps opening a soup can with his talons or dusting his Gibson guitar with his feathers. The one shape that Clark cannot achieve is that of an average young man. He will never have the damsel in the park.

"I thought the ending was touching," Hal said, finishing his juice. "I should take it back today. Any thoughts?"

"Tell him he jazzes the comic book conventions nicely, but Clark's self-pity is annoying. And you're wrong about the ending. Killing off your protagonist is a cheap trick."

"Don't kill him off. Gotchya. Ta, darling."

As Hal turns his Corolla up the hill toward the Miller Hill Mall, he remembers the question about whether a tree falling unheard in a forest can be said to have made sound. More curious, he thinks, is the issue of whether a man, if he makes a statement that his lady doesn't hear, is still mistaken.

Two

At noon, Hal meets Billy, the boy from Electronics, at the food counter. They find a table, and Billy grunts as he scratches near the metal pellet implanted in his nose. His feet barely touch the floor, and he gazes upward at Hal from under spiky brown hair.

"I just wanted to check," Billy says. "I mean, they got nose jobs and implants and stuff. I was wondering what's happening on the chemistry end. They already got steroids. And Viagra. How about pills to change the shape of your whole body? How about pills to zap different body parts? To get a larger chin? You do any research like that, maybe in your spare time? I was asking the other pharmacist, but he zipped his burger trap. Is it a military secret?"

"I'm not a researcher, Billy," Hal replies. "I just sell the stuff. But I don't think the science is that far along." Billy's mouth is too occupied with French fries to protest, and Hal hurries on to praise *Morph Man*, finding a dubious pleasure in telling Billy that Amanda enjoyed the conclusion. "And you're really into all the mania about cosmetics and adornment, about monkeying with the self. There's real sociology in your story!"

Billy forces down his mouthful of fries. "So the drugs are top secret?"

"You could write to the military and ask."

"Write?"

"It's like texting only on paper. They carry it on an airplane."

"Cool."

That evening Hal and Amanda watch the NBC News with Brian Williams, who reports on the latest idiocies and vulgarities voiced by our leaders.

"It's wonderful, isn't it," Amanda says, "how these jerks frame their most ridiculous opinions or most vulgar lies as lapses in style...lapses in linguistic esthetics. They apologize for lacking eloquence, not for lacking humanity or sense."

"Yeah, or the other dodge is to apologize *if* someone was offended. If?"

"Psychologists talk about how everyone invents stories. We all live in our own made-up worlds to some degree," Amanda says. "It's called confabulation. We're programmed to see false positives, not false negatives, so we end up with conspiracy theories—the CIA killed Jack Kennedy, the government bombed the levees after Hurricane Katrina, Obama is not an American. The mind connects dots even where there is no logical connection."

"Timothy McVeigh's dotting killed people."

"Most conspiracy movies and novels are written by people who know what they're doing," Amanda continued. "Dan Brown knows he's inventing conspiracy theories just as entertainment. Well, I assume he knows. But some good artists and writers have cobbled their work out of crazy tool kits. Yeats thought his wife channeled the voices of spirits to him. He was a poet."

"Thank you, dear. I've heard of Yeats. But even Billy at *Target* thinks the military has secret chemicals to change the body."

"There you go."

Later, after giving the evening meal a chance to settle out of harm's way, Hal asks Amanda if she has heard of people collecting body parts via the Internet, something Billy had mentioned.

"It's true," Amanda says, tossing Hal a dish towel and motioning him to get busy. "There was something about it on Nova the other night, along with people who try to operate on their own brains. It's called trapenation or trepenition...something like that. But Hon, I think I'm going to have to limit your Billy time. He's spooky."

In three hours, as Hal prepares for bed before the bathroom mirror, he scrutinizes the hints of gray infiltrating the hair above his ears, wondering if vanity will lead him to chemical solutions.

*

A Procedural Note. If I do not describe the tender labors of the boudoir, the hasty reader should not assume that they are absent from the lives of our protagonists, my friends. These days, opening the cover of a novel is too often like opening the door of a bedroom to confront an epic encounter *in medias res*. I'll adopt the more dignified conventions of an earlier age. After all, we are Hal and Amanda's guests, and courtesy is a higher value than graphic prose. So, before decency is further compromised, let us tiptoe down the hall and bid one another a pleasant *bon nuit,* each retiring to his or her nocturnal beeswax.

*

Two days pass of rain, curdling clouds, and brisk wind, of trees hunching their shoulders and keening, and of people under umbrellas drifting down sidewalks like mushrooms in gray veils of ran. When May unveils the sun again, Hal strolls over to Cosmetics, where local nymphs converge to purchase their potions. He pauses in the perfumed air to invite Shasta to lunch.

As they talk, a scene like one from an embossed cover of a romance novel sold at the checkout line creeps stealthily into his mind. They walk to a nearby park, where a matronly duck and her darlings scurry toward a pond as Shasta chooses a bench in the shade of one of Minnesota's last giant elms.

"Really, he's *way* creepy," she declares. With Shasta things are *so* this and *way* that. Sometimes she wears a green streak in her hair. Way cool. "He's always hanging around Panties trying to get my attention. I can't *imagine* why." Hal fails to respond in the sought-after way, so Shasta continues. "And did you notice that the last time we had lunch here he was sitting across the pond just *staring* at us?" She pushes a straw through the lid of her strawberry shake as Hal realizes that Shasta is the elusive damsel of Billy's graphic novel.

"No," Hal says, "I didn't notice. But don't be too

hard on Billy. He's kind of lonely right now. Someone needs to help him out of his shell." A small man on a yellow moped parks nearby and examines the pond.

From another direction, Hal and Shasta hear, "Hey kids!" It's Waxman from Hardware, finishing his daily half hour of dork-walking around the pond, oblivious of the children who delight in his flailing arms.

"Meltin' those pounds off, Wax?" Shasta calls back. Waxman is a chubby fellow, with a face very like a large bowl of oatmeal.

"Didjya hear the noon news?" Waxman asks, pausing by the bench. "Some kid jumped off the Bong Bridge. Even money it's that goof in Electronics. He hasn't been to work in two days."

"Jesus, Wax," Shasta says, "you don't have to sound, like, *cheerful* about it."

"Sorry," Waxman sings, resuming his Chaplinesque stroll, "didn't mean to sound cheerful."

"He's *so* a ghoul," Shasta declares. She relents, leaning toward Hal and whispering words that smell of cigarettes and Listerine, words that elevate "Weird Waxie" from ghoul to dickhead. "I bet he spends evenings watching reality shows starring idiots." Then she squints at her watch. "We gotta run."

For the remainder of the afternoon, Hal gives mixed-reviews to his romantic, sun-drenched interlude in the park, deciding, as he applies a usage label to a tube of Zovirax, that cheating on your girl isn't all it's cracked up to be.

*

A Shasta Inventory: A curl, coyly straying from its sisters, reclines across her tanned forehead, pointing languidly to the green eyes that, with great frequency, conduct disturbing encounters throughout our sedate city. On her blouse, a button declines its conventional duties, revealing to the vigilant viewer the soft, glandular companions that frolic unencumbered beneath the chic-but-affordable fabric of the blouse that stubbornly refuses to reach its lower destination, thus displaying that currently eroticized scar, the navel, pierced and spangled *a la mode.* Continuing our descent and hastily completing our inventory (lest gentle readers be offended), we will merely note the delightfully snug and fashionably tattered jeans from *Target*'s extensive collection.

*

For the usual reasons of delicacy, the evening television news withholds the name of the deceased. A woman on the bridge, pausing to admire the estuary during her walk from Minnesota to Wisconsin, reported seeing a young man wrestle paraphernalia from a duffel bag, strap it to his shoulders, and disappear over the rail. Judging from his choice of a launch site, he was not particularly interested to land in water. It was speculation, but the investigating officer guessed that the "mess" on the train tracks below included makeshift wings. His statement is all Hal and Amanda need to guess the truth.

"He was like a character in a story," Amanda muses.

"You wonder what elusive sun he thought he could reach. He killed his fictional character off first, and then himself—the fiction was his own story all along."

"Lady Luck was unkind to him," Hal says.

"Isn't 'Lady Luck' God's alias?"

"Or alibi?"

The next morning, a wizened man from Sports tells the inquiring officer that Billy once mentioned an addicted mother in Minneapolis. But two days of official rummaging in that city fail to produce a parent, and on the third day after Billy's plunge Hal passes the hat at *Target* and then drives to a nearby funeral home. There he meets a portly funeral director, hermetically sealed in a gray business suit, starched collar, and blue tie, to arrange for a visitation and cremation.

Later, at Billy's apartment, just a bedroom on a marginal block near Lincoln Park, Hal confronts a blizzard of socks and underwear and a wreckage of pill bottles and lotions. Posters of sports cars and bikini babes cling precariously to torn wallpaper, and from behind the walls dead rodents emit a pungent revenge. Parts of a dismantled cell phone trail across the floor. Hal retrieves *Morph Man* and an ancient Gibson guitar. In two days, these tokens of Billy's life and aspirations are displayed for the 15 or 20 "team members" who brave a rainy night to give Billy's departure a small portion of dignity.

Shasta, the nymph of perfumes and creams, and Waxman, the advisor on hammers and saws, are there, the two drifting into subdued conversation near the donations box. Hushed surmises as to Billy's motivations flutter like moths about the rented and closed plastic casket. Apparently, the mortician despaired at putting Billy together again. The visitation runs its course. The next day Hal places a check in a chubby hand and receives the ceramic vase containing the reduced and dehydrated particles that had been Billy.

Three

It's the day of Amanda's book signing in Somer's Lounge at the College of St. Scholastica, also the day that I first heard the story of Billy. Hal arrives home from work, pausing to place the vase on a shelf of an oak cabinet near the front entrance. He also clutches a dozen roses of repentance.

Amanda is reading aloud to the pictures on the wall. Her book is a collection of short stories, but before reading from it at the college she will offer part of her newest, unpublished story, "The Ambivalent Spring." It begins:

> *It was an April of soft showers lingering in fields and drifting carelessly over hills and country roads. But Carol, viewing the return of spring from the window of her breakfast room, was a realist. The newspaper on the table told of the death of a child, and three days ago, on an evening of crumbling regrets, Carol's father had passed away in the family home in St. Louis.*
>
> *The robin returns to the cemetery, she mused, as well as to the farm, and Chaucer's pilgrims went in search of a dead man. Carol wondered, pouring her second cup of coffee, what commerce her own impending journey would have with death or renewal.*

"That's a terrific beginning, darling—lovely, dark, and deep!"

"The last few days," Amanda says, sitting beside Hal on the sofa, "I've felt like Billy's character in *Morph Man*, Clark, when I write. My computer screen is like his mirror, and I sit there for hours trying to push, pull or slap my experiences into some form that others will want to look at."

"But sweetheart, people *do* look. You've been in magazines. You've done public readings!"

"I have no idea what people see, though...maybe just strange distortions like the forms they'd see peeking in Clark's window."

"Well," Hal concedes, "I have it easier than you. When I sell pills I know that pain and illness will wither and get out of Dodge...a lot of the time, anyway. I suppose it's harder to measure the effect of a story."

"Maybe I'll write about us next."

"Is that what I am? Raw material?"

"Maybe. But, seriously, I wonder if there's anything left beyond the reach of chemistry. We've converted moral failures into medical issues. There's a pill for every atrocity, and we've lost the capacity to make moral judgments. Jesus, *judgmental* has become a bad word."

Despite her anxieties, Amanda's reading goes beautifully. People, including your narrator, form a line such as Hal has never seen at the pharmacy counter; they count out cash or write checks for copies of her book, and a reviewer from *Duluth News Tribune* promises that raves will wash across the region within days. During the signing period, as wine is served, Hal introduces me to a young lady, Martha Gardener, who invites us to a show in a ceramics gallery called *Feat of Clay,* which she manages on the west end of town. After the reading, in a spirit of celebration, Hal and Amanda determine that tomorrow they will visit the newly refurbished *Greysolon Ballroom* on Superior Street. The gallery owner promises that she and her swain will join them. I'm invited too.

Tomorrow arrives with its usual punctuality, and Hal hurries home in the coolness of a late afternoon in May. He pauses on the sidewalk to say hello to a neighbor, Catherine Patterson, who is carrying on a one-sided conversation with her dog, Fritz. Then he enters to find Amanda at the dressing table in the spare bedroom, her personal den of adornment. Hal's roses rise from a vase near the window.

"Hey, this can't be *my* lovely darling," he exclaims, bending to gaze at her in the mirror. Hal's Amanda, he affirms, has beautiful brown hair that curves smoothly to her shoulder. But this Amanda has auburn hair that rises on imagined breezes and swirls about her Grecian features like passion itself. Hal's darling is a natural beauty, whereas this neo-Amanda augments nature with sundry and secret powders and lotions passed down through the centuries from Venus herself.

"Do you like it?" Amanda asks, catching Hal's eye in the mirror. "Am I competitive with that redhead you introduced me to at Billy's send-off, that babe you've been chasing through Ladies' Unmentionables?"

"How did you . . ?"

"Trade secret, sweetie. I snoop to conquer. But answer. Do you like the new me? Am I better than the old Amanda? What's your take on all this artifice?"

"I love both of my Amanda's, old and new." He finds a chair and sits beside her, their eyes meeting in the mirror. On the radio, Bill Evans begins "You Must Believe in Spring."

"Imagine," Amanda says, "he died in a taxi over thirty years ago, but here he is telling us to believe in spring!"

"It's an age of miracles," Hal affirms.

"Let me explain something, Hal. The makeover is more meaningful than natural beauty. Natural beauty is an accident, but the makeover tells a story of inner desire."

"I see," Hal says, "every woman a female impersonator?"

"No, sweetie, every woman a Stradivarius. The mystery of the violin is in the varnish, you know, not the wood."

"Would that woman's music were as soft."

"Let's not debate. Since change is the woman's prerogative, this is the new me. Take it or leave it."

"I'll take it, darling—time and time again."

The mirror is framed with ornately crafted rosewood, almost a carved impression of Amanda's new hair. As "sweeties" and "darlings" fill the air like attendant sprites, Hal and Amanda admire the happy faces that admire them in return. Then he turns his head into the sleeping storm of Amanda's auburn hair.

*

Parting Thoughts: The human character, now a mystery too often fashioned by chemistry, is like a soap opera. Our thoughts, beliefs, and feelings are actors beneath cranial arches, entering and exiting in an endless to-do. Sometimes a beloved belief will leave the stage forever, banished from the script, either by judgment or medication, and replaced by a new performer who may join the cast bellowing and strutting like a bull or creeping silently like a cat under cover of night. Likewise, a particular feeling may be demoted from a central to a supporting role. A person's character, like a soap opera, is never finished—never, that is, until each of us dons futile wings for a final flight.

Will Amanda and Hal live happily ever after? Will their present love maintain its starring role, or will other Shastas be sent from central casting to alter the plot? It's needless to say where our hopes lie, but it is impossible to say what scenes will play in that unconstructed theatre we call the future. A limitation of stories, but one they share with life itself, is that they must always end on this unfinished side of tomorrow.

But while it is still spring and the Bill Evans song lingers, Hal and Amanda smile, dab a few tears, and exchange a prodigious assortment of kisses and snuggles. Finally, after much rearranging of hair and garb, they arrive at the front door, pausing at the oak cabinet to thank the ashes for blessings freely if obscurely rendered. They enjoy an early dinner at *Greysolon*, and then it's tango time. At any rate, that's the story, and some of it is true.

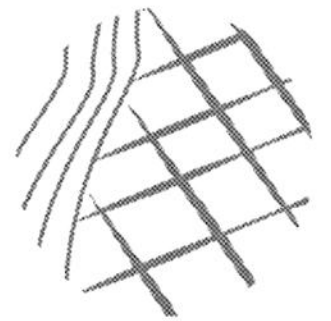

Crooked Miles

"Mother! Alice climbed in the coffin, and Auntie Grace just stood and watched!" It was Brenda in the kitchen doorway yelling at her mother's back.

"What the ...?"

"She climbed in right on top of Grandma! Come see!"

"Jesus Christ ..." Amity had been washing a few dishes in her sister's kitchen. She put down a glass, tossed the towel on the counter, and followed her daughter into the front room, where Grace stood with folded arms watching Alice in the coffin. Roy, Amity's husband, fidgeted uncomfortably in the large brown recliner facing the TV. The Twins were playing the Tigers.

"What is your child doing on top of our

mother! This is outrageous!" Amity's tone echoed Brenda's.

"Your niece is giving her favorite bracelet to our Mom as a goodbye gift. It's a loving gesture. Please keep your voice down." In recent months, no matter what the occasion, ghosts of old rivalries and resentments drifted through the conversations of the sisters.

"Mom," Brenda said, "is Alice . . ?"

"Be quiet, Brenda," Amity scolded. "I'm talking. Jesus, Grace, get her off of there right now!"

"Roy," Grace said to the large man in the recliner, "could you and Amity leave me and Alice alone for a few minutes? We've all had a hard day."

Roy struggled to his feet, groaning like a much older man and mumbling something about the game. He ambled toward the door, motioning to Amity with a flopping forearm. After an exasperated shrug, she followed, turned in the doorway, pointed at the coffin, and asked if Grace intended to "set things right before the relatives arrive."

"I intend to leave things exactly as they are."

When Amity and Roy left the room, Grace approached the coffin.

"The gold star is lovely on Grandma's forehead, and she certainly deserves one. And your favorite bracelet too! Can I help you down now? I see the chair has fallen over."

Amity's indignation made its way to Grace and Alice from the next room: "Just because her husband got himself killed in Afghanistan, she thinks the rules don't apply to her. Whenever we visit here, it's always impropriety and carelessness. She believes in gay marriage! God knows what will become of that poor child. Brenda slept over last month and reported that Alice doesn't even say her prayers! And now defiling the dead? Her own grandmother?" Roy grunted periodically during her tirade, as if to supply punctuation.

"Auntie Amity is mad," Alice said as her mother lowered her to the floor.

"Yes, but you did nothing wrong. Grandma knows you love her."

That evening, after the burial in *Forest Hill* and then the visit to the Veterans Memorial Garden, where Alice's father had been buried recently, Alice asked her mother what Uncle Roy had meant when he called her his "little lay air tease." They were in Alice's room preparing for bed, and Alice wore her pink footie jams.

"Oh, Uncle Roy was just trying to show that he read a Shakespeare play once."

"Shakespeare?"

"He wrote stories to be performed by actors. It was a very long time ago, and in one of the stories a man named Laertes jumps in a grave to say goodbye to someone he loved."

"Can I read it?"

"It's very long, and there are a lot of old-fashioned words. But when you get older, you'll read it in school. It'll be something to look forward to."

"Okay. Look what I have!" Alice said, finding a rose that had slipped beneath the quilt.

"Did you pick that at the cemetery?"

"No," Alice said. "There was a crow looking down and then it flew away and pretty soon it came back and dropped this rose right in front of me. You didn't see?"

"No, I missed that."

"Does Auntie Amity know that kings and princesses used to be buried with treasure?" Alice asked. "I saw it on TV."

"Ah, the Egyptian Pharaohs." Her mother said. "And there was a beautiful Princess named Nefertiti. We could go to the library and find a book about her."

"Okay. Will Grandma see Dad now that she is dead too and they are in the same cemetery?"

"Honestly, darling, I don't know. Would you like to sleep with me tonight and talk about it?"

"No, not tonight, but maybe tomorrow. I heard on TV that they want to give Amity to the aliens."

"That's amnesty, darling. It's a word that means you forgive someone who might have made a mistake. Amity won't be given away."

"She can be too grumpy," Alice said.

"Well, many of us get grumpy sometimes. We have to be generous about it."

"Amnesty for Amity?" She cocked her head like a puzzled puppy.

"Exactly, sweetheart."

In the morning Alice shuffled to her mirror and found a gold star stuck to her forehead. Her first impulse was to call to her mother, but then she smiled and decided to go to the breakfast table in silence, shuffling along in her footies. Grace came from the kitchen, poured orange juice, and sat across from Alice, who could not stifle a smile as wide as summer.

"Well," Grace said, "I see the Gold Star Fairy knows who's been good...her own best helper!"

Alice smiled as she gazed through the window into the front yard, where sunshine poured through the apple tree like lemonade. Leaves shimmered in the breeze, and the old man from down the block came by with his puppy named Lola, who always wore a pink ribbon. It was a new day.

"Mom," Alice asked, "can we talk about dying now?"

"Of course. Would you like to start?"

"Okay."

And so they talked.

Two

Often George and Ruby alighted in an old elm tree in *Forest Hill Cemetery*, where they gazed down and marveled at a statue of a person with wings that stood near the pond with its gazebo and its many geese. Later, hunting nuts or berries by the fence on the upper end of the cemetery, they discussed the strange image. Perhaps it was built to scare away birds such themselves. They had seen such contraptions in gardens, ridiculous assemblages of sticks and cloth meant to stand between them and a meal of berries or corn. But not far from the winged statue was a birdbath, so the scarecrow interpretation made no sense.

And the marble statue had a different feel, elegant and brooding, evoking awe rather than fear. Still, the Corvuses agreed that a human capable of flight would be a bad turn of events, a catastrophe from an avian perspective.

"You could kiss city life goodbye for the rest of us," Ruby declared.

"They'd be too big to sit on power lines," George mused. Agreement did not come easy for him.

"But still ..." Ruby let it drop and began to care for George's feathers.

One day George and Ruby landed in the cemetery to watch people walk slowly among monuments and around the statue and then stand solemnly as a box was lowered into the ground. A small girl cried, and Ruby found a rose to drop in the grass beside her. Later, workmen filled the hole with dirt. The crows decided to return to the cemetery often. Something in the winged statue seemed to invite them, and the birdbath was a plus too.

They returned in the evening to nestle among the leaves and branches of an ancient elm, and the following day they decided to build a nest. Ruby was as happy as springtime itself. The sunlight smelled lush and green, and when they rested they felt like chicks wrapped in summer's golden wing. George was energized, almost his old self again, and they talked through the dawn about materials and design. Would yarn be better than string? Old twigs give a pleasant, rustic effect, Ruby said, but George countered that new ones are stronger and more pliable.

"Maybe we could have a double or two-room nest in case we have guests," Ruby suggested.

"Crows don't have guests. It would be unnatural."

The nest was finished in three days, built from all the materials they had discussed and others that had presented themselves in alleys and backyards. Their first night together in their new home would be magical, and in the late afternoon Ruby felt an old, electric thrill pulsing through her feathers as they entered the branches of the tree. The tombstones stretched away into the darkening cemetery like buildings in a city without lights.

Then, as darkness flowed among the monuments below and the moon was a child's balloon caught in the leaves above, a shape rose from a mound near a new stone. The shape seemed to leak upward from the soil, vague like mist but with the form of a person. It was what remained of an old man, and it moved one way and then another near the mound like a branch keening in the breeze. Finally, it sat on the mound and slowly vanished.

Another evening produced the form of a young woman that drifted among the stones and monuments for a week before growing less substantial as when the shadow of a thinning cloud vanishes. On still another evening a form appeared further off, in an area of the cemetery called the Veterans Garden, where the child had also cried. Ruby leaned close to George on their branch and whispered that she wanted to talk to it. George cocked his head this way and that, and a rising moon came in small pieces through the leaves.

"You," George said. "I talk bad." He had become a crow of fewer and fewer words, and those were not always clear. Perhaps he'd had a stroke. It was a sadness for Ruby. *We're getting old,* she thought. *We are going the way of all feathers.*

"I'll alight on the stone near his mound," she said. "I won't be long. Don't go anywhere, darling. You stay right here. Okaw?"

"Okaw," George replied.

As Ruby planed down and landed, the mist turned to face her. There was something like a human face in it, a vague face as from a dream. Then there were thoughts in Ruby's head that were not her own, and she knew that the form was crying. *Maybe they are not made of mist but of tears,* she thought. *Maybe tears are all that is left when they come out of the ground.*

Ruby stayed for many minutes on the monument as the form swayed before her in the breeze, glowing in the moonlight. His story tumbled like storm clouds in her mind. The form of mist or tears was lost, and Ruby wondered if the winged person made of stone was lost too, lost as hawks and even crows sometimes are in their crooked wanderings.

Far away, an owl asked its ancient question, *who?* Small things hurried in the grass, squirrels to their trees and rabbits to their holes. Ruby returned to the elm to find George dozing.

"It's dead people in the boxes," she said.

"Boxes?" George pulled his head from under a wing.

"The boxes they put in the ground. It's what they do with dead people. They go into a box, like back into a shell, and then the shell goes in the ground by a stone. They call it going on the crow road."

"Why? Crows fly in the air," George complained.

"I don't know, but the bones stay in the box and then the mist comes up from the ground."

"Alive?"

"Sort of."

"Sort of alive?"

"I don't really understand," Ruby confessed. "This one is sad because he was going to come home to see his daughter. But he was at a war and was made dead, so he came home in a box and went into the ground without seeing her. He had gone on the crow road."

"Crow road is stupid to say. What's war?"

"It's when they fight and kill each other. Now that his mist is out of the ground, he will finish going away. That's what he told me."

"Where will he go?"

"I don't know."

"He has to go somewhere," George complained. "Going is always going somewhere."

"Where does the light go when it is gone?" Ruby asked.

"I'm going to sleep," George said.

"And where is that?" Ruby asked. Sometimes she could not resist having the last word.

George folded his head carefully under a wing, and Ruby was left to contemplate what the mist had said about "forever." *How can there be such a thing?* she wondered. Somewhere a cricket chirruped itself to sleep, and the owl repeated its question. Later that night a storm came. The sky ripped to show the fire behind it and in an instant sealed itself, and then the rumbling and crashing began. Trembling, she moved closer to George.

Three

S*ummer* passed. In the fall, the Corvuses always visited Hawk Ridge to watch their cousins migrate. One day, perched in a poplar tree high on the ridge, they saw a freighter in the distance push white ripples aside as it crawled toward the canal leading into Duluth Harbor.

"Water must be so difficult to move in," George said. "Why do they bother?"

"If we were closer," Ruby said, "the ship would move faster."

"I don't understand."

"Neither do I."

They had flown over the hill from their home in *Forest Hill*. The cemetery had become a sad place, and they sometimes needed a change of scene. Now George dozed beside his wife on a branch above the road at Hawk Ridge. Beneath the tree was a garden of fallen leaves, cigarette butts, and candy wrapper.

"I hate all the trash on the ground," George said.

"But some of it is good for us to find," Ruby said. "Stop grousing. They shoot grouse. You're a crow."

"Trash grouses me out."

Sparrows rose from the ground into the trees as if to replace the leaves. The view down the hill to the lake was lovely, what with the many other hills off to the east, all in their autumn reds and golds. It was Ruby's favorite time of the year, even though it meant that colder weather was on the way. But George had become a gloomy companion lately.

Ruby watched nervously as a bald eagle floated high over head, dipping quickly to the ground and then flying off with something in its talons, perhaps a gopher or a kitten or even a dog. She was glad that George hadn't noticed. It would have groused him out too. She and George agreed that there was too much violence. "Sometimes nature just gets by on its good looks," George had said once, when he was young and clever.

Until the past summer, she had not understood where human food comes from, but now she knew that they kept animals on farms just to kill them. And in the autumn, very soon now, they will go out again into the woods with long tubes that make an awful sound and then a deer nearby will lie dying. A human might even rush up to cut it. Autumn is the killing time for humans.

It amazed her that humans are just like some animals, but then, with their cars and tall buildings and airplanes, not like animals at all. And it amazed her that they kill other people for reasons that would baffle a crow or a deer. She understood fighting for food, but for religion or pride? What are they?

"Look, George," she said. "Hawks leaving town for the winter."

After the hawks, an echelon of tundra swans passed, their long necks yearning southward. People along the road stood by their cars and looked at the hawks and swans through things held to their eyes. Every autumn was the same—hawks riding the air down the shoreline and people coming to the ridge to watch. But this time George didn't seem to notice or care. The flight over from *Forest Hill* had been a crooked, difficult mile for him. He had stopped three times and wandered off course twice. "My wings are feathered bricks," he'd complained. Whoever invented the phrase "as the crow flies" hadn't had George in mind. Now, finally, he widened his eyes and watched the other birds, envying their strength and glide.

"Bastards," he muttered. "I'd like to ruffle their plumage."

"But darling," Ruby whispered, "you've always been so beautiful in the air...and in the nest too."

"Caw?" George smiled.

"Caw."

But lately he'd been worried about headaches and sore joints. She remembered how vibrant he'd been, coming to her all in a rush of feathers and flesh in so many small places of sticks, string, and straw...in Hartley Field or Lester Park, at Brighton Beach or in the old cedar tree by the school. Now there would be no more eggs, and she had seen birds lying in the grass, stiff and silent. She was afraid.

A large, black car whispered along the road, and poplar leaves fluttered like small, brilliant wings until the sun went behind the hill to the west, dipping toward the black well to fill itself with more heat as it circled around underneath. The ship was nearing the canal now, and then clouds appeared further off. It was the quiet time before darkness comes smelling of soft feathers as it settles over hills and through branches.

The trees to the west where the sun had gone began to move, nodding and turning to one another as though a serious issue had arisen. Their colorful leaves tumbled together and apart. Ruby knew that they would move the air in their excitement, and soon the trees near her became agitated as well. Branches rose and fell, whispering loudly and causing the air to swirl. From another tree, a flock of red-winged blackbirds exploded into the air and shrunk to cinders swirling down the hill. The light began its liquid slide to evening.

"I was thinking about the little girl who cried in the cemetery, the girl I found the rose for, and then about talking to the mist that was the end of her father. Do you remember?" Ruby asked.

"No," George replied. He had become forgetful.

"We should fly back to our nest," Ruby said. "It'll be dark soon."

"Okaw," George replied, awakening slowly and yawning. "But let's stop at our storage tree first. I want to see our stuff."

Ruby glided lightly from the branch, and George lifted himself stiffly into the air behind her. It was easier to fly when she went first. She'd often carve a path through the wind, but this time he complained of sore wings as it buffeted him about. They alighted by the fallen tree near the visitor's center of *Forest Hill*. Feathers from other birds lay here and there, and tall grass wrapped itself around broken branches. *The broken branches of time*, Ruby thought. They could be words in a sad song, although she had long ago given up trying to learn to sing. All her attempts had been the same caw.

Where the tree trunk had split, there was a ragged hole in which they hid their things. Ruby nudged her head in first, as George stood aside listlessly. It was growing dark, and the wind was cold.

"I think it's all here," she said. "Come and see."

George pushed his way carefully into the hole in the tree and sat down among their treasures, away from the wind. There were two golf balls, many bottle caps, a diamond ring, scraps of paper, a charm from a child's bracelet, a screw, a quarter, aluminum foil, and a collection of feathers. Ruby came and sat beside him.

"Do you remember when we found this one?" she asked, picking up the child's charm. "It was such a lovely afternoon, just a few days after our visit to Wisconsin. We took it as an omen. We were so happy that day!" But she knew that George would not remember.

"I'll sleep here tonight," he said, "with our stuff."

"It isn't safe, darling. We can't sleep on the ground. Foxes, remember?"

They flew to their nest with its view of the Veterans Garden, George pausing to rest on a lower branch before the final ascent. The air smelled of yesterdays as they nestled together. Ruby felt the beating of his heart and the warmth of his body, but she also heard something wild in her own heart, something saying that all of our feathers are autumn leaves.

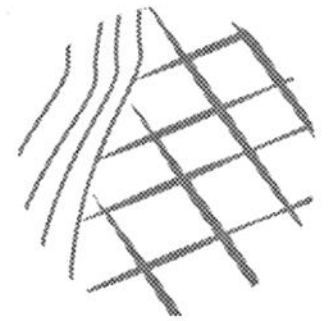

Woven World

Smoky wandered back to the Lake Superior shore often after the flood washed his home down the hill, but now he was finished with the lake. One of the dogs told him the white caps were teeth and the lake was planning to eat him. He wasn't sure about that, but the shoreline smelled of dead things. That was for sure. Dead fish. Dead seagulls. And the other homeless dogs who gathered along the rocks of Brighton Beach were a committee of curmudgeons, lying in the grass or sand yapping and yipping at one another and the world. They seemed to think that each yip, yap, or woof carried deep implications for the future of the planet. *Dumb as a box of kittens,* Smoky thought. *I'm out of here.*

So he headed back into town and up 54th Street in the summer heat, sniffing for p-mail while crows busied themselves around the trash bins at the curbs. He dodged sinkholes filled with puddles like giant tears. One had a car stuck nose down in it. Clouds ambled in from down the lake with its water still brown with mud. When the afternoon rain arrived, a soggy Smoky crept under the awning of a porch attached to a small, yellow house. Eventually the door opened a crack, its chain lock still in place, and he saw part of a woman's head, its gray hair tumbling like mist across an eye.

"Are you a good dog?"

It was tiresome how humans always worried about whether you were a good dog. *No, I'm a great dog!* Smoky wanted to say. Not being able to speak human was frustrating. It was frustrating to have your thoughts locked inside like caged animals, but he gave the trusty old tail-wag that sets people at ease.

"Okay, then," the woman said. Her door closed, and Smoky heard the chain fall. Then the old lady stepped out on the porch. "Do you have a home?" the woman asked. She was a small person in an old-lady dress with pictures of flowers. She wore fuzzy house slippers that looked like rabbits. Smoky sat on his haunches and performed the gaze that follows the wag and completes the job of softening human hearts.

"You look so lonesome, and I bet you're hungry, too. You come in, then, and we'll see what's in the refrigerator. And we have a fan to help us stay cool. Do you like lefsa? Or ham? I bet you're hungry. Did I say that? Sometimes I repeat myself. I say things again. Let me think. Yes, there's still ham!"

He paused inside the doorway to sniff the mail on the floor. He had forgotten about mail slots and their mysterious way of delivering a daily, delightful bouquet of scents. In the kitchen, the woman removed something large from the refrigerator, peeled away the aluminum foil, and sliced some pieces of ham that she arranged on a cracked plate. She bent slowly and placed it on the floor, steadying herself with a fragile hand on the counter. As Smoky made fast work of the ham, the woman drew water into an orange cereal bowl and repeated the laborious process of stooping to the floor.

"There," she said, "that will be your water bowl." Then she picked up a plate that was covered by a towel. "My name is Catherine. Let's go into the living room and meet my friend." It was the first time a human had introduced itself to Smoky.

He followed the lady to where she seated herself on an ancient sofa featuring huge pictures of red and blue blossoms. It was torn in places, and the cushion where the woman sat was concave from use. Her body sank back into the mammoth garden on the fabric, reminding Smoky of a cat he'd known who always backed away into the vegetation. A fan purred as it looked about on a nearby table.

"This is my friend Miriam," the woman said. "She will marry Lyle, my brother, one day when he returns from the war. Would you like a cookie, Miriam?"

The woman named Catherine removed the towel from the plate, which did indeed hold cookies, and offered the plate to the air beside her. *Now that's special!* Smoky thought, cocking his head.

Then the lady picked up a cookie and held it toward him. Her hand was as delicate as an egg shell, and her fingers were translucent. "Open your mouth, and I'll slide one in just like at Holy Communion," she said, her voice at once crackling and sparkling. Smoky eyed the veins of her hand nervously, and then took the cookie. *Peanut butter!* He gobbled it and looked up expectantly as the old lady talked to the air beside her. *Maybe it's weird,* he thought, *but the cookies are good!*

Smoky listened as the old lady explained to the place in the air called Miriam that Tommy visits often because Tommy's aunt, Susan, is single and must work. For a while after the flood, dogs had been able to understand human speech. It was something the wind had blown in—another caprice of nature. But now, Smoky remembered only enough words to decipher some of what was said. He did not know what it meant for the boy to be autistic. Or had she said artistic? He knew that humans like to make pretty things.

"A nice dog will be a wonderful companion for Tommy, Miriam. Tommy lives near where those houses were washed off the hill. It was very frightening for him. His dad just left him there. He pretends to be poor, but really he just didn't want to support his own son. He's tight as wallpaper. You will make Tommy calm and happy," she said, smiling down at Smoky. "And I'll be happy too. Sometimes Miriam is rather quiet, aren't you dear?"

Then she offered a cup of tea to the air. Apparently the air accepted, and the old woman poured tea that was also air into a cup that was air. A less wise dog might have been spooked, but Smoky watched the lady's pantomime with amusement.

"What's that? His name? Now let me see...He's such a pretty brown dog. Fritz! We'll name him Fritz! Here Fritz! Here's a cookie! In giving me you, the Good Lord has kissed my soul on the lips!"

Pretty? Fritz? Smoky took the cookie and weighed the cons and the pros. Fritz sucked. It really sucked. But then what are the chances of finding a human who decides to name you Smoky again? A stray has to go through the naming ordeal. It's the ball you're thrown.

The lady was nuts. Her head was a tree full of birds, and there would be an ongoing problem about whether Smoky was sitting on or in Miriam. On the other paw, the lady seemed kind and an imaginary Miriam would mean more real cookies left for Smoky. Ham followed by peanut butter cookies added up to a very large plus, an excellent way to jump-start a relationship. And although the fan purred and looked about, there were no real cats to scratch your nose. The prospect brightened.

No doubt it would come down to Tommy. *Is he a good boy?* Smoky wanted to ask. It would be nice to help a boy with issues, and Smoky would help if the boy didn't hit him or pull his tail. He knew the advantages of being friendly to humans. "No tail pulling," he tried to say, but all that came out was a whimper.

"Can you sit up, Fritz?" the lady asked, extending another cookie.

Well, here goes. Smoky got his front legs under him and gave her the old, familiar look, the one that makes them think they're gods.

Two

W*hen* Tommy was a child, there was a story about a crooked man. Everything about the man was crooked. Tommy heard the story while lying in his mother's bed, which was also crooked. Then Tommy and his father came north from the big city and the apartment with the crooked bed to the small city by the lake. "Lake Superior!" his father had said, making it sound exciting. But his father only stayed three weeks because he had a calling. That's what he said. It came on the telephone, and Aunt Susan said she hoped it was about a job. She said she hoped he'd send her money.

Now Tommy is the crooked man. The avenue that he lives on wobbles uphill at a funny angle from the lake. The flood ran down the avenue like a river. Tommy climbs this avenue in the late afternoon, sometimes passing the fat lady with her grocery bags. When the old gray house comes into view, it does not stick straight up. It sticks up crooked, and the sidewalk twists and turns through bushes, thistles, and crabgrass. Tommy must be careful climbing the steps to the front door, and then the boards on the porch are crooked. They collide together and bend beneath his feet, making Tommy imagine he is standing in a rocking boat.

A neighbor's house had slid right down the hill in the flood, and he thinks Aunt Susan's house will slide away too because everything about her house is a little off. A little off is what his mother used to say.

"I'm just a little off today, Sweetie. Pass Mama that bottle and them pills like a good boy." Then she would lie back in the crooked bed, pull the sheet to her chin, and close her eyes so that her face was an egg on the pillow.

The ceiling in Tommy's room in the attic of Aunt Susan's home slants down toward the outer wall. Only someone as small as Tommy could stand straight up by the window, although Tommy cannot stand straight because he is crooked thanks to being born that way thirty years ago. He was born a long time ago but is still a boy who can't even have a job. That's what Aunt Susan says and then he cries.

Sometimes Aunt Susan's friend, Catherine, brings her dog, Fritz.

"I brought confections from *Hepzibah's* in Canal Park," Catherine says. "My friend picked them up for me." She opens a small white box tied with a ribbon. "There's one for Tommy, too." Tommy chooses the one made to look like a green pepper. Catherine also brought treats for Fritz.

While the women talk and have tea at the table, Tommy sits with Fritz on the floor. He likes to look into Fritz's brown eyes and to put his fingers into Fritz's brown fur. When Fritz licks his face, he laughs and is happy.

In the early evening Tommy stands at the attic window, which looks into the backyard with all the trees that whisper to one another. He is Humpty-Dumpty, perched high above the ground. If he falls, he will be a broken egg in Aunt Susan's yard.

Further off, the different avenues are lined with houses, and different families live in the different houses. People drag their shadows up the hill like raincoats, and when fog comes from the lake the people become ghosts. Some afternoons, Tommy walks the different avenues when Aunt Susan lets him out. On his own avenue is the blue house where a girl used to live, but now it is just the man that Tommy saw crying on his porch. He wonders where the girl went. On one of the streets, which go the other way from avenues, he saw an ambulance and a person being slid into it like when you slide a stick of gum back into the package. That was after the flood last year, when houses were wrecked.

Some days Tommy walks too long and is late and Aunt Susan scolds and talks about God at dinner as Tommy bends over his bowl and stirs crackers into his tomato soup. The scolding makes him want to go away like his father or like the girl, and he tries to think where he would go. Going is what you do.

When Tommy sits in the bathtub, the tub is the inside of an egg shell, the soapy water is the egg-white, and he is the yoke. He likes to pretend these things and to pretend he is different people inside of the one life in Aunt Susan's attic.

Then, as he snuggles in bed, his thoughts go away. It is strange. They go away turning and turning like water going down the drain. And as his thoughts go, a dark person that Tommy heard of in a story, a person from another country far away where everyone rides on camels, comes through the window in the moonlight to whisper to Tommy about the sadness. The person has cloth wrapped around his head, and he tells Tommy to keep the sadness inside and not let it hatch. If you let the sadness hatch, people will sew up your lips or put buttons on them.

The dark, story person sits in a chair by the window where the moonlight falls on him. After warning not to let the sadness hatch, he gets to the good part. The good part is that if you remember why you are here and do what you are supposed to do, the Great Powers will let you live in a house where the porch is straight, where the floors don't moan at night, and where the attic isn't so hot. But you mustn't be late and make Aunt Susan scold.

The dark person says these things in a low voice. Then he leaves, dissolving into the moonlight like brown sugar in milk. The moon goes away too, and the night is as black as Aunt Susan's Bible. Sleep is a blizzard of darkness.

Birds awaken Tommy with their squabbling. *Hey, fuzz butt, this branch is for robins! No, it's for sparrows!* And so on. Tommy laughs to think what they are saying. He rubs the gummy stuff from his eyes. He knows about the Sandman. Is there a Gumman? Then with the sun rising from the lake and coming through the trees, Tommy is a crooked person in the window watching the birds and further away the whipped-cream clouds that fold themselves together. It is May. Will the mama birds lay eggs? The window is dirty, and one pane has a crooked crack. When Tommy moves back and forth and looks through the different panes, the world outside wiggles like a cartoon.

He pretends that the dust on the window makes

scenes from stories and that the crack is a giant hill. He must look through the story scenes to see the real scene outside. Small squiggles like twigs float in his eyes. There are many things to see through before you can see.

A man standing on the next avenue, pausing as he walks his own crooked mile, might gaze up past the nearest house, past the trees, and through the dusty attic window where a ghostly shape stands and looks down. But if the man were to try to make a story about Tommy, there would be much that he would need to imagine. He would not see from such a distance that Tommy's eyes are lost. He would not see the grief and rage as Tommy tries to remember the comforting words of the dark person in the moonlight. Nor would he hear Tommy's cry. The cry would stay in the attic.

Three

Duluth has lost one of our young men, Kyle Branson, who was killed in Afghanistan and recently buried at *Forest Hill.* He lived down the block from me, and his wife and daughter are still there. I wrote about them in a story set in the cemetery among my friends Ruby and George, the crows.

I see them, Alice and her mom, sometimes as I walk Lola, my brown Shih Tzu. Little Alice Branson can't get enough of Lola, especially when she wears the pink ribbon supplied by the groomer at *Pet Co.* I pray for her future—Alice's, that is. But thinking about Kyle and about his family having to go ahead without him has also made me think about my own past.

My memory is strong today. I've lived in Duluth all my life, except for my stint in Vietnam. I was born in 1941, just before Pearl Harbor. My father survived that war by avoiding it, just as he avoided my mother and me. He was a useless man, hardly worth the dynamite to wake him up. Mom and I had a small house out on Lester River Road that her parents had bought for us when Dad disappeared like a cloud on the horizon. Mom was a nurse, and we did okay, although it was sometimes lonely out there thanks to her work schedule.

We had a maple tree in the front yard, and in back an old chestnut tree lumbered on from year to year. I'd lie by the tree rocking in a hammock strung on a metal frame, and in the distance the green hills rolled away as I imagined the sea must roll in its vast place. During time off, Mom would sit in the grass by the chestnut and read one of the adventures in Oz to me—*Ticktock of Oz, Rinkatink of Oz*, and so many more. I have a photograph of the two of us there.

The picture was probably taken by one of Mom's parents. They visited often and took care of me when Mom was at work. My grandmother, her name was Lillian but we called her Nana, is always old in my memory, battling weeds in the garden and slinging bracelets of water from the hose onto the flowers.

Sometimes she and Granddad would arrive with cookies in the evening, her clothing rustling like leaves, and we'd all sit under the maple in the front yard. We had lilacs, and they were the purple smell of yearly summer evenings. Our roof sported a lightening rod, but TV antennas did not exist. The only satellite was the moon, and the sound of evening was crickets and owls.

As shadows thickened under the maple, we'd listen to a neighbor's German shepherd tethered to a post down the road evoke the failing light with his repertoire of yips, howls, and whines, other sounds of evening. A breeze might sigh contentedly, and Nana might tell a family story, Granddad joking that her memory was so powerful she could recall things whether they had happened or not.

Now I fear that my memory might be of that sort, except that it has nothing to do with power. Occasionally we'd wave to a passing car—a drive-by was a neighborly thing then. There was love despite my father, and my mind works to hold those summer evenings, try as they may to slip away into time's shrubbery.

In the late Forties, there were no concrete swimming pools with all the chlorine you could drink, at least not around here, and on summer afternoons kids would gather at the swimming hole in Lester River by the edge of town. My friend Lyle, his sister Catherine, and I went there often, sometimes just to look at the river that called to us in its strange language. There was something the river wanted to say, and we knew it was lonely in not being able to speak.

Distances called to us too, but it was this place and landscape that defined us, the river, the lake with its ships, the hills we called mountains and talked about visiting one day, trekking down roads under hobo clouds that rode the west wind. But we only splashed about in the river, sending frogs and shiners scurrying, and then sat on the rocky bank, our flesh turned to Braille by the icy water.

You'd warm slowly as the sun reached through the trees to fling gold coins on the stream and as the birds carried on endless discussions in the branches. Sometimes a garden snake would find itself in the rocks by the river, trying to pull itself back into the grass like a thread slipping through fabric. Once, when it was only Lyle and me by the river, a butterfly floated by on a leaf curled up at the edges like a hand holding its delicate rider.

I remember the time, we were in high school then, when we stood not far from the railroad tracks out west of town. A freight train rattled by, dozens of cars in a remote land, and Lyle said it was like time—like history. Each car was an event or a period—a war, a presidency—

and the writings on the cars were headlines. Lyle had begun to see metaphors everywhere, and he might have become a poet had he lived. We didn't know they were our best years slipping by on invisible tracks or a quiet river, and it's strange now to know that my memory of them, even on its good days, is certainly refracted by time's water.

But I do know that we talked once about the future, about what we thought it would be. Later, Lyle died in Vietnam, the war that I came home from with guilt inside like black tar. When I visited Washington a few years later, I found Lyle's name on the Memorial, and the names of others I'd known too, of boys who swim in rivers in no one's memory now, all these decades later.

I visited Catherine, his sister, for a time after returning from the war. You could say we dated. I don't know what she expected of me, or what she knew, but I had loved Lyle. After a few months, she and I retreated into separate shells.

She still lives in Duluth, and we communicate again. I encourage her to call me for any help she might need, and I stop by her house from time to time. Sometimes I bring a box of confections from *Hepzibah's*. We talk about the old days, which she remembers with stunning detail, and I come away with my mind's own pictures of the past dusted off and restored—my first bike propped against the maple tree, shinning and new again, the bottles of cream soda fizzing again in our hands in the summer heat, Lyle's ragged old swim trunks. At other times my memories go vague, losing form like ink in water.

Recently, Catherine took in a stray dog that she calls Fritz. I wrote a story about that, too. Besides Fritz, she copes with loneliness by means of an imaginary companion whom she believes will marry Lyle when he returns from Nam. It's sad to see. On the other hand, she visits an overworked friend with a challenged relative to care for. Catherine brings her dog for the young man's company. And that's good to see. People aren't just one way, and you can't pin them down with words. Nothing is said completely.

When we were kids, things were different than they are now. We listened to *The Shadow* and *Sergeant Preston* on the radio and read *Dick Tracy* in the Sunday paper. We went to Sunday school and learned that *darn* was swearing. Adults bought war bonds, and if they didn't drive a Ford they drove a Chevy. I miss those old days. I'm not saying change is bad or that we should try to climb back over Eden's green wall, but I wonder why we kick the fallen world into ever darker holes. Now we have two or three wars we're fighting at once. There's no path back to yesterday.

I remember my first home out on Lester River Road on summer evenings when a thousand old moments come up out of the fields and forests like insects or seeds to blow across the lawn of my present home. There were trees then where its only buildings now, trees that would turn and swell in the wind after rain.

The man down the road with the German shepherd kept horses, and he let Lyle and Catherine and me walk among them as they grazed. There was a shy one who bowed her head for us to touch. Nothing is prettier in the morning than horses in a field. And there was a pond that a heron visited often, or perhaps it was many different herons, but I prefer to think it was the same one spiraling down from the sky and skimming over the water to assume his one-legged stance. At night the pond was a garden of reflected stars.

These days my joints rub audibly when I move this cumbersome body I've pulled through life, looking back at it and telling it to hurry, roping it and tugging. Now I've been told there are days when my mind is gone, when it doesn't tell my body a thing. When you are old, memories are all you have, hopes and aspirations being the equipment of the young. I care about the young, even after years of teaching school and seeing them in so many lights. I don't tell them what I know to be the truth about most hopes. I only wish them well.

I don't want to die not knowing my own story, which only returns now and then, as it has today, and only in a partial way, an old world of broken threads—a bicycle leaning against a tree, a butterfly held in the palm of a leaf, a blue heron by a pond. Lyle. The past stretches away like the Lake Superior shoreline vanishing around a bend, or like some large but tattered fabric fluttering in the wind. I remember a few of the threads, not the entire fabric. I don't know any other writers, but I think we all attempt to reconnect threads, weaving them into new, imagined places in which the mind can live.

Notes

Actual books, writers, musicians, dictators, and swindlers mentioned in these stories can easily be identified thanks to Google and Wiki. In "Miranda and the Argonauts," Martha's Granny Indiana has the name of a historical person cited in *The Warmth of Other Suns*, Isabel Wilkerson's Pulitzer Prize-winning book on the Great Migration. In the same story is information about North Carolina clay and Josiah Wedgewood's interest in it. This is taken [illegible] from Christopher Benfey's wonderful memoir *Red Brick, Black Mountain, White Clay.*

Information about the life of Bill Evans is from *How My Heart Sings* by Peter Pettinger. In the story "You Must Believe in Spring," Billy's depiction of Clark in his graphic novel is based on a character in John Biguenet's story "Gregory's Fate" in his collection *The Torturer's Apprentice.* And Amanda and Hal's discussion of confabulation was prompted by a chapter in Jonathan Gottschall's *The Storytelling Animal.*

About the Author

Bruce Henricksen taught literature at Loyola University New Orleans, editing *New Orleans Review* for a portion of his time there. He is the author of a study, *Nomadic Voices,* of the major novels of Joseph Conrad, and Bruce's short stories have appeared in a number of magazines. His novel is *After the Floods,* set in New Orleans and in Minnesota, where he now lives with Viki, his wife, who is a potter. Visit Bruce and others at www.losthillsbks.com.

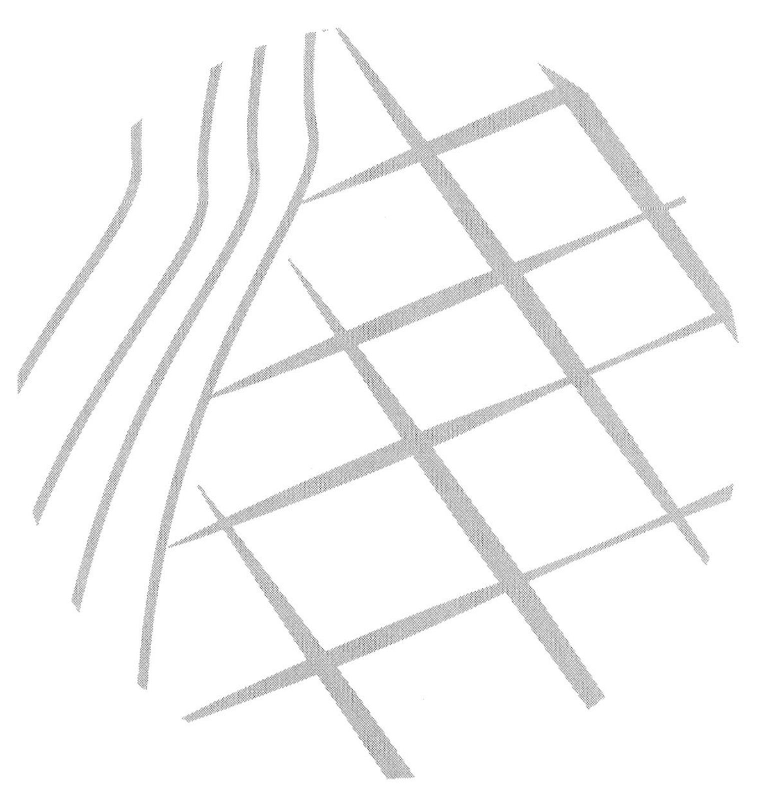